ÐRAGONBOUNÐ
2

White Dragon
REBECCA SHELLEY

Wonder Realms Books

Cover art © 2012 Rebecca Shelley. Cover photography © Paul Schubert, © Lowlihjeng|Dreamstime.com.

ISBN-13: 978-1479300099
ISBN-10: 1479300098

Copyright © 2012 Rebecca Shelley

Published by Wonder Realms Books

To the beloved sled dogs who took me on
many grand adventures.

Prologue

Borealis folded his wings and dove into the ice cave that he and his mate, Saghani, had made their home. Ice crunched beneath his feet as he landed. Saghani looked up at him with hopeful blue eyes. He spread his fore-claws in defeat. It had been so long since he'd found any food, his hunger had given way to a prolonged ache throughout his body and a dizziness that made it hard for him to fly. His wings shook with the effort of getting back to the cave.

I'm sorry, he told Saghani. *The seals are gone along with the sea lions and walruses. Even the caribou and ice bears have migrated elsewhere. The snow wolves watch for me and hide deep in their lairs the moment I leave this cave. If we want something to eat, we'll have to move.*

Saghani let out a weak roar. *You know we can't.*

Borealis eased over to the nest and stuck his nose down into the soft scales where the fragile egg rested. *Do you think it will hatch soon?*

Yes, soon. Saghani stroked the little white egg. *And the hatchling will need to eat right away. Borealis, you must find some food. Maybe if you fly farther.*

I can't fly much more. Borealis lifted his shaking wings. It took so much effort he became dizzy and staggered away from the nest.

Saghani whimpered. Her skin stretched tight against her bones. Her head looked skeletal. The dragonstone on her forehead gave very little light. *There must be something out there to eat. If there isn't enough for you and me, there must be something, be it ever so small, that the hatchling can eat.*

Borealis dug his claws into the ice in helpless rage. *Saghani, I can't find anything.*

What about the humans?

We can't eat humans. They are intelligent beings. Even in the face of death Borealis didn't think he could stoop that low.

No, I don't mean eat the humans. But I've seen them take their little boats out on the water. They pull fish from the sea with their nets and spears. If you went to the human camp, you could get some fish from them. Saghani's thoughts were as soft as an evening wind over a snowbank.

The humans would never give us their fish. If I go anywhere near them, they'll think I've come to harm them, and they'll fight me. We can't talk to them. Humans do not hear dragon thought.

Then take the fish from them without asking. Just fly to their camp, grab the fish, and come back. Saghani lifted her foreclaw to him in supplication. *Please, Borealis, for me. For the hatchling.* She was so near death from starvation it made Borealis's heart ache.

Borealis staggered back out of the cave and leaped into the air, forcing his wings to carry him one last time.

Chapter One

Kanvar's dragon, Dharanidhar, leader of the Great Blue dragons, lowered his head. Kanvar released the leather straps that kept him safe in flight and slid off Dharanidhar's neck onto the charred ground.

Only blackened leaves and stems remained of the Maran Colony's tobacco and cotton crops. The smell of burned greenery rose into the air, and the ashes crunched beneath Kanvar's boots. The colony's great stone gates stood ajar, abandoned by the Maran soldiers that once guarded them. Kanvar's heart twisted.

What have I done? he thought. *My people. I betrayed them. Destroyed them.*

4

Dharanidhar snorted. *They weren't your people. You are Varnan not Maranie. Besides, we didn't kill anyone. We just burned their crops, caved in their mines, and sank their timber flotillas. You were right. As soon as the colony started losing money instead of making it, the Maran soldiers and colonists left all on their own. No more fighting. No more killing. You didn't destroy them. You saved them.* Dharanidhar let out a deep laugh and thrashed his tail, sending up puffs of ash. His sightless eyes glittered with glee.

Kanvar covered his mouth and nose with his arm and squinted to protect his own eyes from the ash as he limped away from Dharanidhar and slipped through the gates, dragging his crippled leg behind him. His stubby left arm swung uselessly at his side.

Inside the deserted colony, Kanvar licked his lips then wished he hadn't when his tongue came away with the ash's caustic taste.

The volcanic stone buildings rose like jagged pieces of darkness, defying the hot sun that burned overhead. Moisture condensed on the stone, and sweat soaked Kanvar beneath his mismatched armor. At one time, Kanvar had been used to the heat and humidity, but he'd spent the last few months in the high mountains with the Great Blue dragon pride, only coming down to visit his friends, Tana and Raahi, in the village and keep his promise to train Raahi as a dragon hunter.

Kanvar's feet carried him first to the army barracks where he'd spent five years indentured to the old soldier, Chandran. Though he knew it was impossible, he half-hoped to see Chandran there.

Kanvar tensed, expecting a gentle reprimand for arriving so late and failing to polish Chandran's armor.

None came. Chandran's quarters were as empty as the rest of the colony. A ruby dragonfly buzzed around the room and landed on the windowsill. Sunlight glinted through its jewel abdomen. Its wings stilled for a moment, then it thrashed its tail and zipped outside.

"Chandran," Kanvar whispered as he ran his fingers along the stone table against the wall. It had served as desk, workbench, and dinner table for him and Chandran. "Father." Yes, Chandran had been more of a father to Kanvar than a master.

"I'm here."

Kanvar jumped at the sound of the crisp voice from outside. He retreated from Chandran's quarters and stepped out of the barracks. A man stood across the street. The breeze tossed his golden hair and glinted off the crown that rested on his brow. His skin was bronzed from the sun. He wore a shimmering golden robe over a white silk shirt and tan pants.

Kanvar flinched back against the barrack's rough stone walls. The last time he'd spoken with the Great Gold King, Amar, his father, Kanvar had defied him. His father had seized control of Kanvar's mind and body and tried to stop him from bonding with Dharanidhar instead of one of the Great Gold dragons his father had picked out for him.

Amar spread his hands. "I'm not going to hurt you."

Kanvar shuddered and secured the strongest shield he could muster around his mind to keep his father out.

"That's not necessary." Amar folded his arms and remained at a distance.

"What are you doing here?" Kanvar forced his voice to sound strong. "I told Indumauli to ask Devaj to come alone." Indumauli was a Great Black serpent who had saved Kanvar's life once. Kanvar had trusted him to get a message to his brother, Devaj.

"You're my son. Did you think I wouldn't want to see you, to talk to you? I know things have been a bit rough between us, but it doesn't have to stay that way. I care about you, Kanvar. Please . . . let's talk this out."

In the back of Kanvar's mind, he felt Dharanidhar dig his claws into the ground and growl.

Amar's dragon, the Great Gold Dragon King, Raja-hansa, had been Dharanidhar's enemy for a long time. But now that Dharanidhar was bonded to Kanvar, the two dragons had agreed to an uneasy truce. Kanvar glanced around the deserted colony, though he knew Rajahansa would be invisible in the burning sunlight. Dharanidhar would have preferred to know Rajahansa's location, just to be on the safe side, and Dharanidhar relied on Kanvar's eyes to see.

"He's on the building right behind me," Amar said.

Kanvar reinforced the shields around his own mind.

"I don't need to read your mind to know you are looking for Rajahansa. Tell Dharanidhar we came to talk, not fight."

"Talk. Of course. Because Rajahansa knows Dhar-anidhar would win with both wings broken and one claw tied behind his back." Great Blue dragons were fighters. It's how they lived, how they made their place in the pride. In contrast, Great Gold dragons were scholars and artisans. And yet for all recorded history, the Great Golds had ruled, kept in power by their exclusive bond with Nagas like Amar. Kanvar had broken every dragon law and tradition by bonding with a Great Blue.

Amar grimaced. "I suppose Dharanidhar would win, but that's not the point. The point is I wanted to see you. To make sure you are all right. To tell you how proud I am of the Naga you've become."

Kanvar straightened and stepped away from the wall. He could hardly believe what his father had said. For months he'd feared his father's wrath for bonding with Dharanidhar. Nightmares of his father yelling at him had more than once woken him in a cold sweat. "Y-you . . . you're not angry?" He didn't dare let himself hope.

A firm hand clapped down on Kanvar's shoulder. "Hey, little brother. You're looking good, considering the vile company you've been keeping."

Kanvar jumped and reached for his crossbow. His right hand closed on empty air, and he remembered he'd left it in Dharanidhar's cave, not expecting to need it for a visit with his brother.

Devaj stepped back. "Pretty good reflexes." He slugged Kanvar on the arm. "But lousy observation skills. You let me come up right beside you without even noticing. Are you a dragon hunter or not?" A wide grin split Devaj's face, and his eyes sparkled with good humor. He dressed and looked very much like Amar, except for the air of fun that hung about Devaj and not his father.

"Well," Kanvar spluttered. "I was—" He waved his hand at Amar who kept his distance across the street.

Devaj laughed. "Any excuse will do, but that would not keep you alive if I were a rapacious green serpent."

"Devaj." Kanvar's throat tightened. The last he had seen his brother, Devaj had nearly died. Only a powerful elixir had restarted his heart.

"Kanvar." Devaj grabbed him in a tight hug. "You saved my life. Twice."

"Three times at least." Kanvar returned Devaj's hug. A warm feeling swelled inside him. He was glad to see his brother alive and well. "And I don't keep vile company. The blue dragons are majestic and loyal friends."

Devaj stepped back, rested both hands on Kanvar's shoulders, and stared into his face. "Thank you, Kanvar. You risked so much . . . gave up so much to save me."

Kanvar looked down and twitched. He knew Devaj meant that Kanvar had given up bonding with one of Rajahansa's sons and offered himself to Dharanidhar instead in exchange for Devaj's life. But Kanvar didn't feel like he'd lost anything by bonding with Dharanidhar. His bond with the Great Blue dragon was so much more fulfilling than he had ever imagined possible.

"I didn't give up anything," Kanvar choked out. "I gained a great treasure. One I'm very happy with."

Devaj rubbed a smudge from his robe, left by Kanvar's ash-speckled armor. "I'm glad you're happy, little brother. Father and I have been worried about you. Has Dharanidhar been treating you all right?"

Kanvar grimaced. "He was a bit rough at first, on accident, not on purpose. He didn't know he could hurt my mind, but we've worked that out now."

Kanvar didn't mention the first night after they had bonded when Dharanidhar had forced him to eat raw meat. Dhar had simply not known humans preferred their food cooked.

Devaj nodded. "Neither of you have any training. You should return to the palace with us so Parmver can help you."

Parmver was an ancient Naga who had rescued the royal line when the Great Blue dragons led the slave revolt at Stonefountain a thousand years before. Kanvar liked Parmver and wouldn't mind seeing him again, but Dharanidhar growled in the back of Kanvar's mind. *They say they want to help us, but when we got there, they'd never let us go free again. They might even try to break our bond and force you to bond with one of them.*

"N-n-no. I won't go back to the palace." Kanvar shuddered and headed toward the gates, putting more distance between himself and his father, though he doubted he could move fast enough to get away if Rajahansa decided to grab him.

Devaj kept pace with him. Not hard since Devaj had two good legs and Kanvar a twisted, crippled leg that always dragged along behind him. "Kanvar, I don't know what Dharanidhar just told you, but I'm betting he's wrong. Father and I only want to help you, not hurt you in any way."

Kanvar looked over his shoulder and found that his father had made no move to follow. A glance at the rooftop showed no ripple of gold that would mean Rajahansa had taken flight. Kanvar forced himself to limp faster. He might get away after all.

"Kanvar wait." Devaj caught hold of his good arm and forced him to halt. "All right. Forget the whole idea of going to the palace. I'm sorry I suggested it. At least tell me why you wanted to talk to me before you run off again. It must have been important, or you wouldn't have sent Indumauli with the message."

Kanvar swallowed hard and pulled away from his brother's grip. A swarm of jewel dragonflies zipped in and out of the open shop window where Kanvar had once purchased his crossbow. The shop stood empty now except for the glint of color refracted through the dragonflies. Their wings filled the air with a soft buzz. Kanvar wiped the sweat out of his eyes and faced Devaj.

"I-I've been having nightmares. Grandfather Raza is in great danger. We've got to find him, bring him back, and restore his memories before it's too late." The vivid image of a Great White dragon loomed up in Kanvar's mind. Swirls of frost clung to its translucent wings. The dragonstone in its forehead blazed a blinding white. It blew a blast of frigid breath at Kumar Raza, and Raza froze solid, killed instantly by the cold.

"Kanvar." A gold heat warmed him and wrapped protectively around his mind, forcing the nightmare back into his memories. He felt Devaj's hand resting on his forehead and the silky thread of Devaj's thoughts in his own mind. Kanvar's mind shields had failed when the waking nightmare had enveloped him.

Kanvar gasped and pushed his brother away. "Leave me alone. Don't do that."

Devaj's thoughts vanished from Kanvar's mind and the warmth with them.

DRAGONBOUND

Kanvar shivered despite the hot sun in the sky. "You saw, didn't you? Grandfather is in trouble and it's father's fault. He sent Grandfather Raza on a quest to kill the Great White dragon, without his memories, his training, his weapons or armor. Father wants Raza to die."

"Father doesn't want any such thing. He sent Grandfather away to keep you and me safe after Grandfather found out he was a Naga. It was the only way." Devaj glanced back toward Amar and then returned his gaze to Kanvar. "Please, little brother, our father is a good man, a kind and gentle man. I don't know why you continue to believe the worst about him. He loves you and would do anything to keep you safe."

"I don't want to be safe. I want my grandfather back. If father cares about either Grandfather or me, he'll tell me where to find him. He knows. Ask him for me, Devaj. Please. Convince him to tell me where Grandfather is, so I can go get him."

Devaj frowned.

His sudden sternness surprised Kanvar.

"Kanvar, even if you found Grandfather. Even if you saved him from the Great White dragon. The moment you unlocked his memories, he would turn against you. He would kill you without thinking twice. You are a Naga. Dragonbound. Enemy. The most reprehensible of all living beings to him. Kumar Raza will never accept you and love you the way father and I do."

"Never mind," Kanvar said. "I knew father wouldn't help me, but I thought you might." Kanvar's heart felt as heavy as his useless left leg as he limped away. Maybe Devaj was right, but it made no difference. Kanvar vowed to find his grandfather anyway, save him from the Great White dragon, and restore his memories.

"Kanvar," his father called from behind him. "He's with the Tuniit tribe. They roam the coast of the Great North between the Varnan colony at Illulissat and the Teniteqilaq Sound."

Kanvar twisted back to stare at his father.

Amar nodded at Kanvar. A ripple of gold swooped from the building, picked up Amar, and glided away. A second ripple snatched Devaj from the street and followed the first.

Kanvar grimaced. His friend, Raahi thought the Great Gold dragons' ability to remain invisible in direct sunlight was the best of the dragon traits. It gave Kanvar the shivers. He sagged against the closest building. The rough stone pressed into his armor. The shrill call of birds and chatter of black monkeys wafted from the jungle and bounced between the deserted buildings. Watching his father and Devaj fly away left Kanvar feeling as empty as the streets.

That went well, Dharanidhar rumbled in Kanvar's mind. *They didn't try to blast me with their joy breath and drag you back to the palace. They told you exactly what you wanted to know. So what are you upset about?*

I don't know, Kanvar answered. *Father and Devaj are my family. I just . . . wish I could figure out how to get along with them.*

Dharanidhar sent a ripple of comfort through Kanvar's mind. *Your Grandfather Raza is family too. Maybe after you've saved him, you'll feel better about your father. Now come on. I can't stand here all day waiting for my eyesight back.*

Kanvar pushed himself away from the wall and headed out the gates. At least he wouldn't be alone in his search for Kumar Raza. Dharanidhar would go with him and help him.

Chapter Two

Ðenali paddled the seal-skin boat to the frozen shore. Choppy waves slapped the sides of the boat, and dark clouds crowded the sky. An arctic wind whipped tiny ice particles into his face. A storm was on its way, and Denali knew he had to get off of the water.

Only a few dragonfish flopped about in the net at the bottom of the boat next to his fishing spear. The dragonfishs' tails and wingfins were stumpy and deformed, and none of the catch were larger than Denali's palm. It wasn't enough to feed even his own family, let alone share with the tribe as custom required.

ÐRAGONBOUND

Denali scanned the faces of the fishermen who had come to shore before him, but could tell from their pinched looks that their catches had been the same.

A group of seal hunters approached the camp from the far side, their spears slung over their shoulders, their hands empty. The fluffy gray dogs slunk along at their heels. Denali's father, Kumar, led the seal hunters. If there had been any seals anywhere within a week's walk, Kumar would have found and killed them.

Denali drove a walrus-tooth spike into the ice and secured the boat, then jumped out, hauling the net with him. He carried the fish into camp, past the thick hide tents that made up his people's homes. In the center of camp, they'd constructed an icehouse for storing the tribe's food. Denali climbed the ice steps to the top and emptied his net.

Atka, the best fisherman in the tribe and the man who had taught Denali to fish, climbed up onto the icehouse. He carried his fishing spear and two sea serpents. Their frosty scales glinted in the Great North's perpetual half-light, but they were both shorter than his forearm.

Denali had seen Atka bring a whale to shore once that could have swallowed the whole village. The Tuniits had feasted on its blubber for almost a year.

Atka's face wrinkled in disgust as he dropped the stunted serpents into the icehouse. He pushed his fur-lined hood back and scratched his head. The cold wind tried to tear his shiny black hair out of its braid. "I don't know, Denali. We must have offended the sea spirit somehow. Almost all the fish and animals have gone.

Those that remain are . . . well . . . like that." He gestured toward the hole.

Denali fished his last piece of blubber from the pouch slung over the shoulder of his seal-skin jacket. He twisted the greasy blubber in his hand. "We're going to starve to death, aren't we?"

Atka stared out across the frozen land. "No. We won't starve. We'll move. We'll search until we find what we need to survive."

"We've already moved the camp a dozen times this season. Every place we go the hunting and fishing get worse." Denali shoved the blubber back into his pouch. His stomach rumbled with hunger, but he figured he better save the blubber. He might need it later.

Kumar strode to the center of camp and thrust his spear into the icy ground. "We found no sea lions or seal holes. We'll have to move," he shouted. He needn't have bothered. The women were already dismantling the tents despite the dark storm clouds overhead.

Denali climbed down to stand beside his father.

The senior members of the tribe gathered around Kumar. They had no official leader, but most often Kumar came up with the best plans and the tribe chose to follow his advice.

"We've hunted everywhere already," Kapik said. He was the oldest member of the tribe. Many of his great-grandchildren were Denali's age. He was as wrinkled and tough as hardened leather.

Kumar ran his fingers through his frozen beard, tugging off the ice crystals that had formed there. His skin was whiter than the rest of the tribe, and he alone seemed able to grow such a thick beard. "I think we'd better go to Illulissat. I know that the food the Southerners bring in their big boats won't make our people strong like seal meat, but it might keep us alive until the animals return. We have some seal skins we could give in trade for the food."

Tartok, who had been Kumar's rival for the love of Denali's mother, spit on the ground at Kumar's feet. "You are still a Southerner at heart. Of course you would suggest we go to Illulissat. But they will not help us. They think we are no more than animals ourselves."

Angry mutters broke out between the men. Soon shouting followed, until Kapik let out a piercing whistle and waved his spear in the air, forcing the men to silence. "Since we cannot agree, we will have to consult the women for a final answer."

The women heard Kapik's announcement and gathered around. It did not take them long to agree among themselves. For the sake of the children, the tribe would follow the coast down to Illulissat. They went back to their packing, securing everything in the boats or on the sleds and harnessing the dogs for travel.

The men broke apart to go help, except Tartok who shoved Kumar in the chest. "It's you. It's your fault. We should never have let you join us. The sea spirit is angry and punishes us because of your presence."

"That's not true." Denali kicked the butt of Tartok's spear, sending the weapon spiraling out of his hand.

Tartok grabbed the front of Denali's jacket, lifted him into the air, and shook him.

Kumar pressed the head of his spear against Tartok's throat. "Put my son down."

Tartok dropped Denali and walked away. Denali scrambled back to his feet, rubbing the ice and snow off his seal-skin pants. An angry heat burned his chest and face. "Why do you let him talk like that?" he asked Kumar. "He could turn the whole tribe against us."

Kumar snorted. "Nobody listens to Tartok, but you'd better stay away from him. Come on now, we've got to go help your mother pack. The tribe will divide the fish up when we're ready to go."

"Kumar!" Atka called down from the top of the icehouse. "I think you should come see this."

"What?" Kumar pulled his spear from the ice and bounded up the icehouse steps. Denali followed.

Atka pointed out across the ice. Denali squinted but couldn't see anything other than snow blowing across the ice ahead of the coming storm.

Kumar's hand tightened on the haft of his spear. "It can't be. I've spent twelve years hunting for a Great White dragon and found no trace."

"I think perhaps it is," Atka said. "And it's coming toward camp."

A column of snow condensed and spun along the ground in the distance. "That's a dragon?" Denali asked. It was said that anyone who caught sight of a Great White dragon would be blessed for the rest of their life.

Kumar sucked in a sharp breath. "Even if it is a Great White, it wouldn't come near us. They're too reclusive to bother the camp." But as he spoke, the swirl of frosty white sped closer.

Atka grabbed Kumar's arm. "The dragons live on sea lions and seal meat the same as we do. We haven't found any all season. Only the fish have kept us alive."

Kumar grimaced. "White dragons don't fish. Their wings are too fragile to dive below the surface."

"Right," Atka nodded. "The only thing available for the Great White to eat right now is us."

The swirl of snow stopped within range of the camp and burst apart, revealing a Great White dragon. Ice crystal patterns clung to its translucent wings at it spread them wide and reared up on its hind legs. It opened its jaws, revealing sharp icicle-shaped teeth. It roared, and the ground shook.

"Cover your eyes!" Kumar shouted.

His hand wrapped around Denali's face, blocking his sight a split second before a bright flash lit his father's hand with a red glow.

Atka let out a sharp cry.

The light vanished.

Kumar twisted Denali to face away from the Great White dragon and dropped his hand from Denali's face.

Water streamed from Atka's open eyes and froze to ice on his cheeks. "I can't see."

"The light has blinded him," Kumar said in a thick voice. "Help him down, Denali. Get your mother in the boat and leave. Don't look back."

Kumar's words sent icicles through Denali's heart. "What about you?"

"I'll follow with the dogs and sled. Meet you at Illulissat. Now go." He nudged Denali toward Atka. Behind him, Denali heard the crunch of the ice as the Great

White dragon advanced on the camp. Cries of fear rose up from the tribe. The dogs let out terrified howls that subsided to whimpers as the dragon grew closer.

Denali grabbed Atka's hand. "Come on. This way."

"The crystal. So beautiful. So bright," Atka mumbled. "Like a star plucked from the sky and placed in the dragon's forehead."

"The dragon blinds its prey before attacking," Kumar called. "Nobody look directly at it. Just get out of here, everyone. Go quickly. I'll keep its attention on me."

Denali guided Atka down the steps of the icehouse and over to his boat. Atka's wife and sons were already aboard with all their possessions. They helped him into the boat and shoved away from shore.

"Denali." Eska, Denali's mother, wrapped a protective arm around his shoulders and dragged him to their boat. He dropped to his knees and held it against the ice shelf, pulling his fishing spear out of the way as Eska climbed onboard.

"Come on," Eska said. "Hurry."

Denali set one foot down in the boat and pulled the sea lion tusk free of the ice, ready to push off.

A roar like the sound of a glacier splitting off into the water made his ears ring. He glanced back and saw his father still on top of the icehouse, waving his spear, and taunting the Great White dragon with a shrill whistle.

The Great White shot toward him in a swirl of ice and snow. It towered above the icehouse so Kumar stood barely as high as its chest. At the last moment before the dragon reached him, Kumar threw his seal spear, but the

Great White dragon flapped its wings, creating a gust of wind that sent the spear spinning away harmlessly.

"No!" Denali shouted. He lifted his foot out of the boat and used it to kick the boat away from shore.

"Denali," his mother screamed and tried to paddle back for him, but Atka's wife grabbed the side of her boat and held it while his two sons paddled with all their strength away from shore.

Denali raced back toward the icehouse. He couldn't let his father face the Great White dragon alone. The crystal in the dragon's forehead glistened with amazing beauty, catching Denali's eye and dragging his gaze up to stare at it.

Kumar drew his hunting knife, pressed his arm across his face, and half-turned away from the attacking monster. Denali remembered his father's warning at the last second. It took all his will to tear his eyes away from the beauty of the dragonstone before the blinding white flash split the sky.

The sound of ice crunching and scraping followed the flash.

Denali looked back and saw that the Great White had torn the front off of the icehouse. The tribe's pathetic catch slid out at the dragon's feet. Altogether it would hardly be more than a mouthful for the Great White. The dragon filled the air with another ice-rending roar, fixed its hungry eyes on Kumar, and sucked in an icy breath.

Denali skidded to a stop at the base of the icehouse. He whistled and waved his fishing spear to get the dragon's attention the way his father had done. The Great

White dropped its gaze to Denali and shook its head as if it couldn't believe such a small boy would fight it.

"That's right, look at me, you monster. I'm not afraid to fight you!" Denali screamed. At the same time he threw the spear. Not at the dragon, but up to his father.

Kumar caught it, raced forward, and leaped off the icehouse at the dragon.

Chapter Three

The Great White dragon lowered its head toward Denali just as Kumar jumped. With the full weight of Kumar's body behind the spear, it sank deep into the dragon's chest.

Denali let out a triumphant cheer.

The Great White dragon roared and clawed Kumar away, flinging him aside. Kumar crunched to the ground on the far side of the icehouse.

The dragon tried to breathe a spray of icy air at Denali, but its breath came out in a gurgling gasp. Then its eyes glazed over. A crackling sound filled the air as its body crystallized into ice. Denali could hardly breathe as he watched the Great White dragon transform from a living creature into a towering ice statue, majestic, even in death.

Denali's feeling of triumph vanished. Tears filled his eyes, and he rubbed his chest. It felt like a piece of his own heart had died with the Great White dragon.

A groan tore Denali's attention away from the dragon. He ran around the back of the icehouse to the far side. His father lay crumpled on the ice. The front of his seal-skin jacket was torn, and blood welled up from four gashes left by the dragon's claws. Denali raced over and whipped off his own jacket to press against the wound, staunching the flow of blood.

"Denali," Kumar's eyes fluttered open and he grabbed Denali's hands. "Take my hunting knife and use it to get the dragonstone." Blood trickled from a gash on the back of Kumar's head where he'd hit it when he fell.

"The dragonstone?" Denali's hands shook as they held the jacket against his father's chest wounds. The biting wind swept shards of ice against Denali's bare back. He shivered with cold.

"The Great White dragonstone. The Southerners will pay anything for it. The tribe will have enough food for years. Enough to survive until the fish and seals come back."

"But—"

"I'll be all right for a moment." Kumar pried Denali's hands away from his chest and put pressure on the wound himself. "Go get the dragonstone."

Denali backed away. Blood dripped from his mittens, making his grip on the hunting knife slippery as he picked it up. The wind intensified, and the dark clouds dropped lower to the ground.

Reluctant to leave his father, Denali climbed to the top of the icehouse, stepped across to the shaft of the spear imbedded in the ice dragon's chest. From there he climbed up to the dragon's shoulder, plunging the knife into the ice as he went and using it as a hold to draw himself up. The frozen dragon was so cold it felt like liquid fire against Denali's bare chest as he climbed. The dragon's head was lowered since it had been looking down at Denali when Kumar speared it. Still, Denali had to stretch as far as he could to reach the dragon's forehead.

Using the knife he chipped the ice away from the stone until it slid free into his hand.

He tucked it in his pouch and climbed back down to his father. Kneeling, he held the dragonstone out for Kumar to see. It was six inches long and two wide. Clear, with symmetrical facets.

Kumar blinked up at the dragonstone, then pulled his mitten off, reached up and took it out of Denali's hand. As soon as his bare hand wrapped around the stone, his body spasmed. He cried out and gasped, squeezed his eyes closed, and then blinked them open. They focused on Denali.

"Who . . . who are you? Where am I?" Kumar said.

"What do you mean, who am I?" Denali cried. "I'm your son, Denali. And you . . . you've been hurt. We've got to take the sled and catch up with the rest of the tribe. Kapik will know how to treat these wounds."

"No, but wait, I have a daughter not a son. Her name is Mani. Where am I?" Kumar tried to rise, but fell back when he tried to move his leg. Denali's jacket slipped loose, and blood seeped from the dragon scratches.

"By the Fountain," Kumar swore, pressing the jacket back against the wound with his free hand. "Those will have to be stitched. Do you have a steel needle and cotton thread?"

Denali shook his head. "Stay there, father. I'll get the dogs and the sled. We need to go."

Kumar caught sight of the frozen dragon above them. His eyes widened as if he hadn't known the Great White was there. He looked from it to the dragonstone in his hand. Then his eyes glazed over. "Amar," he cried out. "Amar, please. No, wait!" His body jerked again and he fell unconscious. The dragonstone slipped from his limp fingers and skidded away across the ice.

Denali replaced his father's mitten then retrieved the stone, tucked it in his pouch, and raced to where his family's tent had stood only minutes before. The tent and whale-bone poles were wrapped up and tied onto the sled along with a bundle of Kumar's things. Eska had packed their other possessions on the boat. Kumar always drove the dog team.

The dogs whined and pawed at the snow as Denali approached. They were still staked out, since Eska hadn't had time to harness them. The harnesses and lines were in a pile on top of the sled. Shivering, Denali untied the pack and pulled out his father's extra jacket. It was big on him, but he rolled up the sleeves and snuggled into the warm fur.

As soon as Denali picked up the harnesses, the dogs broke into excited howls. They hated to be left behind when the rest of the sleds had gone.

Denali peered down the sled tracks, but could see no sign of anyone. The tribe had gone, and gone quickly. A glance out to sea showed all the boats out of sight as well. Denali was alone with his unconscious father. He knew how to hitch the dogs to the sled, he'd done it plenty of times, but that didn't help his sudden feeling of abandonment and fear.

A vast expanse of white wasteland spread around him. It was his home, and yet suddenly it wasn't. His home was the tribe, the camp, the tents, the smell of burning seal oil and boiling serpent meat, the sound of children laughing, women scolding, and men boasting of their hunting prowess. All that was gone, and only ice and snow remained.

Swallowing his fear, Denali bent over to slide the harness onto the lead dog, Iluq.

Iluq licked his face and whined, then bolted toward the trail the other sleds had left in the snow. He only got a few feet before reaching the end of his tether.

"Stop that," Denali scolded him. "You have to let me harness the others first."

He got the harnesses on the other seven dogs, but only hooked two of the dogs up to the sled to start. Miki and Niki were the two biggest and his father's favorite dogs. Their muscles strained as they lunged against the lines, but the sled remained in place, secured by a whale bone snowhook, anchored deep in the ice.

Denali got a firm hand on Niki's harness before he pulled the snowhook free. He knew the dogs would bolt for the trail, anxious to catch up with the rest of the tribe. They tried it and almost succeeded, despite Denali digging his feet in and attempting to turn them back toward the icehouse. They dragged him for a couple of yards before his shouts and tugs brought them around.

Sweating and breathing hard, Denali led Miki and Niki over to his fallen father, then put the snowhook back down and jumped on it to drive it into the ice. The dogs howled and pulled, but couldn't break the sled free from the anchor.

Gritting his teeth, Denali loosened some of the ties that held the tent to the sled and went over to his father.

Kumar's face was pale. Blood slicked the snow.

Denali knelt and used the ties to tighten his jacket against Kumar's chest. That seemed to stop the bleeding, and Denali turned his attention to Kumar's right leg. It was bent wrong, and Kumar had been unable to stand on it. Broken most likely. Denali forced the leg straight, wincing at the sound of bone grinding against bone as he did. He used two of the shorter tent poles to splint the leg, then tried to lift his father onto the sled.

Kumar weighed too much.

Denali groaned, wishing he were older, bigger. Wishing at least one other man of the tribe had shown enough courage to stay and help fight the dragon.

Niki yipped and doubled back on the line to get to Kumar. He pawed at the blood-soaked ice and licked Kumar's face.

"Good idea," Denali said. He untied Niki's line from the sled and wrapped it under his father's shoulders.

"Come on boy." Denali grabbed Niki's harness and guided him toward the front of the sled. The dog's toenails dug into the ice, giving him traction, and he dragged Kumar up to the sled.

Denali patted the bundle tied to the top of the sled, and Niki jumped up.

"Good, now come on. This way." Denali pulled Niki forward so his paws rested on the handbar at the back of the sled. "Come on, Niki. Jump."

He tugged on Niki's harness.

Niki jumped over the handbar and off the back of the sled. The rope tightened and pulled Kumar onto the sled.

"Good boy. Good boy." Denali buried his face in Niki's warm fur and rubbed the dog in appreciation. "I couldn't have done it without you."

His success in getting his father onto the sled encouraged him. He had the dogs, the sled, the tent, his father's hunting knife. Denali looked around. His father's seal spear lay a few yards away where it had fallen when the Great White dragon had deflected it. And the tribe's small catch of fish and serpents spread around the dragon's feet.

Denali untied the line from his father and secured Niki to the sled. He retrieved the spear and bundled the fish up in a seal skin, then tied everything down to the sled, including his father.

He had a bit of a struggle getting the other restless dogs hooked up. They were strong and anxious to run and dragged Denali from their stake-outs to the sled more than he led them. At last all eight dogs spread in a fan in front of the sled, howling and lunging against their lines. Iluq had the longest line and would lead the others, hopefully responding to Denali's commands.

But Iluq was Kumar's dog, and considered Kumar pack leader, not Denali.

Taking a deep breath, Denali stepped up onto the whale-bone runners at the back of the sled, got a tight grip with one hand on the handbar, and used his other hand to tug the snowhook free.

The sled shot forward. The sudden rush of wind against Denali's face stole his breath away. The dogs loped across the ice, following the tracks of the other sleds, kicking up bits of snow as they went. The wind howled across the open expanse, and the first flakes of snow stung Denali's cheeks.

The other sleds of the tribe had hugged the shoreline, staying close to the boats, but moving fast to get away from the Great White dragon. Denali couldn't understand how they had gotten so far ahead though. The fight with the dragon had not lasted very long. Of course he'd taken time to climb up and get the dragonstone, and treat his father's wounds. But the tribe couldn't be that far ahead. Besides, with a storm blowing in, they wouldn't go too far. They'd want to set up the tents before the worst of the storm hit.

In the Great North, day and night had little meaning. In the winter, the sun never quite tipped up above the horizon, leaving the land in perpetual twilight. In the summer, the sun rose in the spring and stayed low on the horizon until it set in the fall. Kumar had told Denali that in the south the sun rose and set in twenty-four hour periods. Denali had a hard time grasping the concept. The Tuniits slept when they got tired, and woke when they'd rested. Denali fought to stay awake while the dogs carried him into the biting wind. He'd rest when he caught up with the tribe.

The darkness deepened as the snow fell thicker. Denali lost sight of the trail left by the other teams. It lingered somewhere beyond the veil of snow that obscured his vision. He could only see the length of the sled and the tails of the dogs that pulled it. But the dogs kept moving. They could smell the trail and would follow it to the new camp.

Kumar had often told Denali, when you cannot see, you must trust the dogs. Now Kumar lay limp and silent on the sled. Snow clung to the edges of his fur hood, and ice crystals encrusted his beard.

Frozen flakes gathered on Denali's eyelashes, and he brushed them away every few moments as he squinted into the sheet of falling snow ahead, looking for the dark smudges against the ice that would be the tents of the camp. He could barely hear the sound of the dogs panting and the sled sliding across the ground, but he strained to hear the sound of voices carried on the wind.

Instead, he heard a rumbling sound.

The ground shook.

"Iluq, stop!" he shouted and grabbed the snowhook from where it hung on the side of the sled. "Stop! Iluq!"

The rumbling grew louder.

Iluq put on a burst of speed, unwilling to stop before rejoining the rest of the tribe.

Denali reached down and tried to catch the snowhook on the ice, but the sled was moving too fast for him to stomp it into place.

All his efforts only slowed the sled a little.

"Iluq!" he screamed. "Iluq, gee." Since he couldn't get Iluq to stop, he hoped the dog would at least follow the command to turn to the right and head inland.

Iluq let out an angry howl and pressed forward as if he'd caught the scent of the camp close by.

A terrible cracking sound rent the air, and the ice beneath the front dogs split apart. Iluq and two others went over into the sudden chasm.

Their weight jerked the sled forward. The other dogs fanned to the left and the right, but Denali could tell they wouldn't be able to hold back the heavily loaded sled at the speed it was going.

Snowhook in hand, he jumped from the back of the sled, landing with the snowhook points down beneath his chest. The weight of his body drove the whale bone into the ice. The snowhook made a horrible squealing sound as it was pulled forward, but finally it held.

The tip of the sled hung over the edge of the rift.

Denali jumped up and ran to the front of the sled, slipping and sliding, dodging the remaining dogs and lines. Three dogs dangled down in the chasm. The sound of churning water came up from far below.

"Iluq." Denali grabbed Iluq's lead line and tried to haul him up, but Denali didn't have enough strength or weight to do it.

He grabbed Miki and Niki's lines and wrapped them around the lines of the hanging dogs and tried to get Miki and Niki to pull them back up.

Both dogs tried, their feet scrabbling on the ice. But their tug pulled the front of the sled to the side and partially dislodged the snowhook. The sled slewed around and tipped toward the ice rift, threatening to spill Kumar into the chasm.

Chapter Four

"No!" Denali screamed as he, pulled the hunting knife, and lunged to the front of the sled. Tears streaming from his eyes, he sliced Iluq's and the other two dogs' lines.

The three dogs fell, yipping in fear, and splashed into the torrent of frozen water far below.

The sled righted itself and came fully around behind Miki and Niki. Denali grabbed the front of the sled and helped pull it back away from the rift.

The remaining dogs were a tangle of lines and feet and fur around the sled.

Miki and Niki growled and started a fight with two of the other dogs as if blaming them for not helping. Denali had to kick all four to break them apart.

"Stop it!" he yelled at the dogs. "Stop it. We have enough trouble."

He went to the snowhook, reset it, and jumped on it until it was deeply wedged in the ice. Then he crawled to the edge of the rift and stared into the eerie darkness below. There was no sign of Iluq and the other dogs, just the roar and gurgle of rushing water. Denali's heart twisted. He'd lost three of his father's dogs.

Shouting in frustration, he climbed to his feet and stared across the chasm. A big chunk of glacier had calved into the sea and created a rift, cutting deep inland. With the thick blowing snow, Denali couldn't see anything on the far side of the rift. The Tuniit camp could be over there just out of his sight.

He whistled and screamed and waved his arms, then listened for a reply. Only the howl of the wind and grumbling water answered.

Denali stumbled back to the dogs and gave each of them a reassuring rub before dropping to his knees beside the sled. His father had tipped on his side, but remained unmoving and eyes closed. Denali pulled a mitten off and wriggled his fingers down past his father's hood to his neck and felt for a pulse. It was faint, but there.

"Father," Denali said, shaking Kumar. "Father, wake up. I've lost Iluq. He's gone. I can't get to the camp, and I don't know what to do."

Kumar remained limp.

Denali buried his face against his father's arm. The ground grumbled and shivered.

"Oh no." Denali jumped to his feet. "No. no. no," he muttered as he tried to untangle the dogs as quickly as he could. He was still too close to the sea and the unstable ice. With his heart flapping like a dragonfish in a net, he pulled all the dogs around to the front of the sled and set them facing inland. He'd have to go that way until he reached the edge of the rift, then he could pass it and come back out to look for the tribe on the other side.

After getting the dogs pointed in the right direction, he ran back to the sled, and tried to pull up the snow-hook. It stuck, frozen in deep where he'd set it. He pulled with all his might, but couldn't work it free. The ground rumbled and shook.

Desperate, Denali used the hunting knife to chip at the ice around the hook. The dogs milled back on their lines to face across the chasm the way the trail had gone. One of them started a forlorn howl, and the others answered. While Denali stabbed the ice with the hunting knife, he strained to hear an answering howl from the dogs at camp.

The wind rose in fury, whipping an ever thicker wall of snow into Denali's face. He could make out only the sound of his own dogs.

Finally he got the snowhook free. He tapped it down just a little bit into the gathering snow on the ground and hauled the dogs back around the direction he needed to go. When he walked back to the sled, the dogs followed him, whining, and turning in circles as if ready to bed down for the night.

"No!" Denali yelled at them. "We have to go. It's not safe here. Come on. Hike." He gave the command for them to run, but they ignored him.

Groaning, Denali pulled the snowhook free, hung it on the side of the sled, and trudged to the front. He grabbed one of the dog lines, unhooked it from the dog and double-tied the dog on one of the other lines. Then Denali put the free lead-line over his shoulder and pulled.

The sled barely budged.

"Come on, Niki, Miki, help me." He pulled again. Again the sled hardly moved. But Niki and Miki shook themselves and came up beside him.

As soon as they pressed into their harness and snapped their lines tight, the sled started forward. The other dogs reluctantly followed.

With Denali in the lead, and the dogs helping pull, the sled moved inland into the teeth of the raging storm. As long as Denali walked out front, the dogs kept moving. As often as he tried to go back to the sled, the dogs stopped, and sank to the ground. But Denali didn't want to stop. His father was too hurt, too weak. Storm or no storm, Denali had to get him to camp. If that meant detouring inland around the rift, then he'd do it.

He put his head down against the wind and snow and forced his body to move, step by step. Always forward. Swimming through the blizzard. Staying where he could see the rift as a black line to his left. Watching it gradually thin. Soon he'd be able to get past it and turn back out toward the sea.

Beside Denali, Miki lifted his nose and sniffed. He let out an excited howl and bolted forward. The other dogs followed. The sled almost hit Denali as it shot after the suddenly loping dogs.

Denali jumped to the side at the last moment. If he hadn't been holding onto one of the lines, he would have been left behind as the sled raced away.

The momentum pulled him off his feet. He slammed to the ground, clutching the line, dragging along on the snow and ice.

"Stop!" Denali shouted. The dogs ignored his shouts for a few minutes before finally slowing enough that Denali could struggle to his feet and catch hold of the handbar of the sled. He drew himself up and put his feet on the runners.

The dogs kept pulling straight inland. They'd picked up some kind of trail. Denali hoped it was the path the tribe had taken.

The rift disappeared behind him, and he lost all sense of direction in the dark swirling snow. He dozed. How long he wasn't sure. But he snapped wide awake when the howling wind vanished and the flying snow fell away behind him.

He looked around, but was surrounded by darkness. The dogs stopped, turned in circles to make themselves a sleeping place, and settled to the ground.

Denali stamped the snowhook into the ground and backtracked until he could hear the wind and see the snow flying just beyond a crack in the darkness. The dogs had brought him safely into the shelter of an ice cave. Denali ground his teeth and walked back to the sled. The dogs hadn't been following the tribe's trail at all. It was some other trail, probably of a creature that made its home in the cave.

He worked the fishing spear loose from the tie downs on the sled and drew the hunting knife. He'd come too far inland to think the dogs had been smelling seals or sea lions. Whatever creature lived here, Denali knew he had to be ready for it. No coaxing or yelling he did would get the dogs moving again until the storm ended. At least he was out of the wind and snow.

Denali crouched down beside his father and waited, nerves tense, ears strained to hear the sound of some creature in the cave.

The howling wind echoed through the cavern. Now and then the faint sound of ice cracking punctuated the raging storm, but nothing approached. Gradually the wind outside fell silent. The dark clouds lifted, letting in the pale half-light. The dogs remained curled with their fuzzy tails over their faces. Denali stood and surveyed the cave.

With the light filtering in, he could see it was much bigger than he first thought.

The jagged ice walls towered above his head. The light coming in from outside tinted the ice in shades of blue and green, accented with crystal patterns. Only a few feet in front of the sled, a giant outcropping of ice protruded into the middle of the space. From where Denali stood, he couldn't see to the top of the protrusion.

He shuffled back a few steps to get a better look. His heart gave a sudden surge like the sea before a wind-storm. The form that filled the middle of the cave was not just a random bit of ice, sculpted by wind or water.

It was a Great White dragon.

Majestic and beautiful, and frozen to ice. A female dragon. Her face was narrower than the dragon that had attacked the camp, and her eyes were kind. She lay curled on a nest of soft scales she must have plucked from her own body. Her translucent wings were lifted as if she'd tried to get up just before she died and turned to ice. The frost patterns on the wings were the most beautiful Denali had ever seen.

He only needed one look to know what had killed her. Her hide was shrunken tight against her skeleton. She'd died of starvation.

A feeling of utter loss filled Denali. He let out a wail and sank to his knees.

His mind tumbled like snow on the wind. Her mate had come to the camp, but he hadn't attacked any member of the tribe. He'd headed straight to the icehouse. Denali had thought his father had lured the dragon there, but that was wrong.

The Great White dragon had been trying to steal the fish to take back to his mate. Denali knew it in his heart as he stared up at the dazzling beauty of the she-dragon above him.

Other than trying to blind those who tried to stop him, her mate had not hurt anyone until Kumar drove the spear into its heart. But even if Kumar had not killed the dragon, there weren't enough fish in the icehouse to save its mate.

"I'm sorry," Denali said. "I'm so, so sorry."

He sheathed his hunting knife and went to his father. The white dragons were dead, and he couldn't bring them back. The he-dragon Kumar had killed would have died of hunger soon anyway, just like its mate.

Kumar lay wrapped up tight on the top of the sled. Sweat glistened on his face. His eyes were still closed.

"Father?" Denali shook him gently. "Wake up. I don't know where we are, and I'm not sure how to find the tribe. Father?"

Kumar's eyes fluttered open, but remained unfocused. "Rajan, I'm going hunting," he said in a slurred voice. "I know you're sick, but I'll find the gold dragons. I promise. . . . Will you leave him here to die? . . . No. Don't shoot. Don't shoot him, please."

Kumar struggled against the straps that held him to the sled.

Denali loosed them, fearing his father would hurt himself in his fevered delirium. Nothing Kumar said made any sense.

Kumar slid from the sled and pushed back his hood. His blurry eyes looked up at the Great White she-dragon. He gasped and stared transfixed and shaking.

Denali noticed the back of his head where it had slammed against the ice was swollen even worse than before. Blood still trickled from the gash. "Father?" Denali knelt to get a better look at the head wound. It was bad. No wonder his father was delirious.

"I don't know what to do with this. I've got to get you to Kapik," Denali said. "Climb back up onto the sled, we need to go." He lifted his father's arm over his shoulder and tried to guide him back onto the sled, but Kumar pulled away. He tore his feverish eyes from the dragon to look at Denali.

"Devaj, what did you do to your hair? Why has it gone black?" Kumar ran shaking fingers over Denali's braided hair.

"I'm not Devaj, whoever that is. My name's Denali, remember? I'm your son." He nudged his father's hand away and undid the straps holding the seal-skin jacket against the wounds on his father's chest. They had started to scab along the edges, but blood still seeped from the deep scratches. No wonder his father was fevered. With a sinking heart Denali realized his father would die, if he couldn't get him to someone who knew how to care for his injuries.

"Denali?" Kumar said as if he'd never heard the name before. "Denali, my son? Amar you foolish man. If only you would have listened. Denali, where are we?"

"The Great White dragons' cave." It hurt Denali to think his father had forgotten who he was.

Kumar coughed, pressed the jacket back against his own chest, and tightened it down. "I'm dying, Denali."

"I know." Denali rubbed the moisture from his eyes so it wouldn't freeze his lashes shut.

"When I'm gone, find Amar if you can. You may need him."

Denali shook his head. "Don't talk like that. I'm not going to let you die. There's still time if I can find the camp. Come on. Get back on the sled."

With Denali's help, Kumar struggled onto the sled, but the effort cost him, and he fell unconscious again as soon as he lay back.

Denali whistled to wake the dogs from their sleep. The five remaining dogs stretched, shook themselves, and stared up at Denali with expectant, hungry eyes.

"Well I don't have much," Denali said. He unwrapped the dragonfish and handed one to each of the dogs. His stomach complained. He would have loved to save all the food for himself and his father, but he knew the dogs were the best chance he had to survive and rejoin the tribe. He hoped, despite the storm, they would be able to follow their own trail back to where the fissure in the ice started.

The dogs finished the fish in one gulp and whined for more. Denali kept one out for himself, wrapped the rest back up, and secured the bundle to the sled. "Sorry. We have to make it last."

Denali scrapped the scales off the fish and devoured it almost as quickly as the dogs had. Just as he chewed the last mouthful, a sharp crack came from the nest beneath the she-dragon. Denali tossed aside the fish bones and crept toward the nest. Lots of things made cracking sounds—bones breaking, ice breaking, boats breaking. None of them good. Another big crack was followed by softer crackling.

Readying the hunting knife in one hand, he hooked his other arm over the lip of the nest and pulled himself up to see inside. There were only a few inches between the frozen she-dragon and the edge of the nest. A pair of big blue eyes seemed to fill the whole space. They looked up at him and blinked.

Denali shouted in surprise and dropped to the ground. In a mirror response, the creature in the nest let out a surprised squawk.

A pearlescent claw appeared at the top of the nest, digging sharp talons into the scales. Then a second claw. There was a scrabbling sound and then a sleek white dragon head snaked over and peered down at Denali. It was small, smaller than Miki. Feminine, like a miniature of the dead she-dragon that sat on the nest.

The baby dragon mewled at Denali, than scrabbled some more with its hind legs, and managed to flop out of the nest at his feet.

Denali jumped back. His heart pounded like the icy sea against the shore.

A baby. Mucus still clung to its wings and body.

Just hatched. It blinked its big eyes up at Denali and mewled again.

And hungry. Not so different than the dogs whining for food.

It flapped its little wings and wobbled toward Denali, opening its jaws to show tiny but sharp teeth.

The clear stone on its forehead pulsed white, stinging Denali's eyes. He looked away and blinked, grateful the hatchling hadn't flashed its light as bright as its father had when he attacked.

The light was too bright for comfort, anyway, and Denali hadn't been ready for it.

When he looked back, he found the baby dragon had crossed the distance between himself and the sled and was using its claws to tear away the jacket from his father's chest.

Denali shouted and dove for the sled just as the dragon's long white tongue snaked out and hungrily licked at the blood that seeped from the wounds.

Denali tried to stab the little monster, but it hopped to the other side of the sled and continued to feast on his father's blood.

"No. Get away."

Denali swiped with his hunting knife and managed to scratch the dragon's muzzle.

It let out a sharp cry, licked the cut, then flapped up, grabbed the packet of fish, and swooped away to the far side of the nest behind its frozen mother.

"Hey, that's my food," Denali complained. He re-secured the seal skin against his father's chest, snatched up the spear, and took a few steps back toward the nest.

The she-dragon's eyes seemed to stare down straight into his heart. With the baby dragon's mother and father both dead, the catch it had taken from Denali would probably be the only food the little dragon ever got before dying of starvation like its parents.

"But I don't want to starve either," Denali whispered. Still he could not force himself to go after and kill the little dragon. He shook his head and called for the dogs to come around and face out of the ice cave. For once they listened to him. He pulled up the snowhook, and the sled jerked into motion.

Chapter Five

Kanvar leaned tight against Dharanidhar's neck to protect his eyes from the cold wind as Dharanidhar flew.
They'd followed the Kundiland coast northward for two
days, leaving behind the steamy jungles and skimming
over evergreen forests, the air getting colder and colder
as they pushed toward the Great North.

The sun set. The further north they went, the shorter
each day got. Dharanidhar snorted and glided down to
land on the rocky shoreline.

Great waves thundered against the rocks, sending up
a violent spray that stung Kanvar's cheeks.

"I don't want to make camp here," Kanvar said. "It's too cold." His armor had always been warm enough in the high mountain meadows where the blue dragon pride nested. Here it felt like only a flimsy piece of fabric, incapable of blocking the biting wind.

Dharanidhar took flight again, hugging the coast line, searching through Kanvar's eyes for some place more sheltered. He found a small bay with quiet beaches and a sheltered grotto.

He swooped low over the water and into the grotto. The overpowering stench of rotting fish and marine life blasted Kanvar in the face. A cacophony of grumbling, grunting, and barking filled the air of the wide cave, and Kanvar looked down to see furry brown and gray bodies lining the rocky shore and swimming in the water. As soon as Dharanidhar flew into the grotto, the creatures below let out terrified yaps, dove into the water, and raced out into the bay.

Three of them were too slow, and Dhar snatched them up in his front claws before settling onto the vacated rocks.

Sea lions, Dhar said, quite pleased with himself as he dispatched the sea lions he'd caught and shoved one of them whole into his mouth. *Smelly, but tender and juicy. When I was younger I'd fly up here once in a while just to hunt them. Worth the effort too, but I've never seen so many here before.*

Kanvar didn't complain. He was hungry. They hadn't spent much time hunting during their flight.

Dhar skinned the smallest one and roasted it for Kanvar with a breath of hot blue fire. Kanvar got out his knife and cut himself a fat-drenched slice. "Why so many do you suppose?" he asked between mouthfuls.

Don't know. I think the biggest colonies are along the Great North coast. Perhaps they've migrated here for some reason. Dhar polished off his second sea lion and settled down on the rocky shelf overlooking the water.

Kanvar filled his stomach and then scooped some of the water into his mouth to quench his thirst. "Oh, that's cold," he said, shaking the water droplets off his fingers. So cold it had felt like ice going down his throat.

You want to fly out and gather some wood for a fire? Dhar asked.

"No thanks." Kanvar settled down between Dhar's forepaws. "I don't want to stay here very long. I have such a bad feeling in my gut that we're going to be too late to save my grandfather."

The dogs pulled Denali and the sled across the snow-swept ground. They were following some trail Denali couldn't see. He hoped it was back to the fissure, but he was disappointed hours later when the broken icehouse and the frozen Great White dragon his father had slain came into view. Since the dogs had been unable to reach the tribe the day before, they had brought Denali back to the last place the tribe had camped. Their instinct had led them home, but the camp was no longer there, and the site had changed.

A whole stretch of the ice shelf had broken off into the sea, leaving steaming black rocks behind.

"But it's not spring." Denali stamped down the snowhook and walked to the shore.

A half-dozen dead dragonfish floated in the water, lapping up against the rocks with each rippling wave.

Denali took his mittens off and scooped them out of the water. The dogs whined and howled for food.

Ignoring them, Denali knelt and stuck both hands back down into the water. He was used to the sea's biting cold, but the water wrapped his hands in pleasant warmth. Heat from the rocks he knelt on penetrated his thick fur clothes. Seaweed rippled just below the surface in the warm current.

Denali whipped off his jacket, got out the hunting knife, and reached clear to his shoulders into the water to cut the delicate plants. He needed food badly, and couldn't pass up this chance to get as much as he could.

Deeper out, a yellow-orange glow lit the water, giving Denali a hollow feeling of dread while he harvested the seaweed.

When he'd cut all he could reach along the shore he put his jacket back on, bundled the seaweed, and carried it and the dragonfish up to the icehouse. Food left out in the open and unguarded never lasted long. He packed the meat and seaweed into the front of the icehouse where the dragon had torn it open. He reached for the blocks of ice back to cover and secure the food. As he did, he noticed some places where the ground had been clawed up and yellow marks here and there on the ice blocks at the bottom of the icehouse. Denali sniffed the yellow spots, wrinkled his nose, and backed away.

A pack of snow wolves must have caught the fish scent from the open icehouse and come to investigate. The wolves had marked the empty cache as their own.

Denali scanned the horizon for any sign of the pack. Snow wolves would not usually bother humans, but then neither did Great White dragons. He'd have a much better chance fighting the feeble baby dragon than a hungry pack of snow wolves.

Denali's body ached from all his exertion. He hadn't slept at all during the storm. He was exhausted, and had to keep going in search of the tribe, but the icehouse was the only defensible structure around.

To the east he saw movement across the white expanse. One spot then two. Then a half a dozen and more. If he left now, he might be able to stay ahead of the wolves, but the path the rest of the tribe had taken was gone. Melted away by the hot stones near the shore.

Shuddering, Denali grabbed the bundle of food and hurried to the sled.

He was surprised to see his father's eyes open as he wrapped the seaweed and fish in a seal skin.

"Rajan." Kumar grabbed Denali's arm. "Rajan. You've been shot. Stay here. I'll go tell father there's been an accident." Kumar was awake, but his mind was lost in delirium once again.

"There's a pack of snow wolves coming," Denali said. "Do you think we should stay here? We might be able to hold them off from the top of the icehouse. Not sure if we could keep all the dogs safe, but we could try. Or we could run for it. Maybe stay ahead of the wolves."

Kumar blinked up at him. "Snow wolves?"

"Yes, snow wolves."

"You mean black monkeys?"

"No. Snow wolves. Come on, get up. I think we'd better stay here and use the icehouse."

Kumar rolled to the edge of the sled and tried to stand but cried out in pain as soon as he set his feet on the ground. His eyes seemed to clear. "My leg. What happened?" He ran frantic fingers over the make-shift splint Denali had used to stabilize it.

"It's broken. Let me help you. If we can just make it to the top of the icehouse, we should be safe." Denali wrapped his arm under his father's shoulders and tried to help him stand.

Kumar got to his feet, but fell back onto the sled panting before even taking a step. "It's no use. I'll never get to the top of that building. Whatever it is."

"Right." Denali gritted his teeth and secured his father and the food to the sled. He got the dogs pointed westward than pulled the snowhook. "Hike now. Come on boys, run."

The dogs lowered their tails and sniffed the ground. They felt they'd come home and were not eager to leave a place they knew well.

"Hike," Denali yelled. He grabbed some snow in his hand, balled it up, and threw it at Miki. "Go, stupid dog."

Miki laid his ears back and growled, unwilling to take orders he felt were wrong from a human pup.

"Hike!" Kumar's deep voice boomed out.

The dogs snapped into a lope. Heaving a sigh of relief, Denali leaned against the handbar.

"Why won't the dogs listen to you?" Kumar asked.

Denali shook his head in frustration. It was like his father had become a different person. "I'm too little. They don't respect me." He leaned over and touched his father's shoulder. "You seem to be feeling a little better. Why don't you know me? Can you remember anything?"

Kumar reached up and gripped Denali's hand. "I remember in the ice cave you told me you are my son. I know there is a Great White dragon back there with a spear in its heart. Did I do that?"

"Yes." Denali glanced behind him for sign of the snow wolves in pursuit but could no longer see them.

Kumar tightened his grip on Denali's hand. "The dragonstone. We need to go back for the dragonstone."

"We already have it. It's here, safe in my pouch." Denali pulled his hand away and patted the pouch. "But if we didn't have it, we couldn't go back. Those snow wolves are hungry. You're hurt, and I'm not big enough to fight them.

"How old are you?" Kumar asked.

Denali winced. He was small for his age, and hated that. "I'm almost twelve."

Kumar grunted. "Twelve years. Amar, I'm going to kill you when I get my hands on you."

Denali ignored his father's rant and pulled the last of the seal blubber from his pouch. "You must be hungry. Here." He handed it up to his father.

His father grimaced. "What's this?"

"Food."

"You call this food?"

"Just eat it."

Kumar put it in his mouth and chewed for a moment, then spit it out. "That's revolting. I'd die before I could keep that down."

Denali stared at his father in horror. He'd wasted a whole chunk of blubber. The very last that they might get in a long time.

"Don't look at me like that," Kumar grunted.

Denali refocused his eyes straight ahead.

The dogs pressed forward, following the shore, but staying off the rocks. Denali scanned the horizon for signs of the fissure. He didn't want the dogs to go over the edge a second time.

"What's your mother's name?" Kumar asked in a softer voice.

"Eska." Denali could barely choke out his answer. The smash on the back of his father's head must have done some serious damage for him not to remember the woman he cared so deeply for.

"A beautiful name." Kumar sighed and unfastened the make-shift bandage from his chest to check on the dragon claw wounds.

"Uh, Denali? You didn't tell me you had a stash of Great Dragon saliva packed somewhere on this sled."

Denali glanced down at his father and let out a sharp cry of surprise. The gashes on his chest had healed over, leaving behind four livid red scars. "What kind of spirit magic did that?" A shiver of fear went through Denali. He'd never seen any wound heal so quickly.

Kumar rubbed his hand across the puckered skin. "It's not magic. It's dragon saliva. I know the smell and feel of it, believe me. But if you didn't apply it, who did? I thought we were alone out here, though I have a feeling we shouldn't be."

"No. We most definitely shouldn't be. Especially with a hungry pack of snow wolves behind us." Denali glanced over his shoulder, but still couldn't see the snow wolves. The dogs had fallen to a steady trot, a pace they could keep up for hours.

"But dragon saliva, where did it come from?" Kumar shivered and flipped the jacket around to the opposite side which was less covered with blood.

Denali bit his lip as he thought about the baby white dragon. He'd been so sure the horrible creature wanted to eat his father. But it had licked the wounds and not taken a bite out of Kumar's unprotected body.

"You going to tell me?" Kumar said gruffly.

Along the shore, a large patch of ice slid hissing off the rocks into the warm water. The dogs adjusted their course to run a bit farther away from the sea.

Denali cleared his throat. "There was a dragon egg in the cave. It hatched. Little thing. Clumsy and delicate. It flashed its stone at me and then attacked you. At least, I thought it meant to eat you. It was licking your chest, and

I drove it away with my hunting knife. The little beastie stole all our fish."

"That's strange. If it was hungry, you'd think it would have gone for the fish first. Not that I'm complaining." Kumar rubbed his chest then lay back and closed his eyes.

"Does that mean you're going to be all right?" Denali said, hopefully.

Kumar groaned. "I don't know which hurts worse, my leg or my head. But at least I'm not bleeding to death now. I think we owe that little dragon my life. Don't know why it did it though. Must not have understood I killed its parents."

"You killed its father. Its mother died of starvation. Something's wrong. All the game has vanished. The ice is melting. The rocks are hot. I've never seen anything like it before."

Kumar didn't respond.

Sometime later, a black line appeared ahead where the fissure blocked their path. The dogs slowed. Denali dropped the snowhook, and the sled jolted to a stop.

Kumar cried out and clutched his head. "Ouch. You should warn a person before you stop like that."

"Not funny," Denali said. "Look."

Kumar opened his eyes and squinted at the line where the ground opened into the chasm. "What is that?"

"It's a big ugly hole in the ice that could kill us. The glacier flows down to the sea here." Denali felt strange explaining something to his father that his father had taught him years before. But with his father's memory gone, Denali needed to make sure Kumar would help him get the dogs around the rift safely.

"The glacier was smooth and flat here. Our tribe has used this snow bridge safely my entire life, but yesterday when I came this way in the storm, that huge fissure opened up right in front of us. Iluq, Kaper, and Aga fell in. I wanted to get them out. I tried, but you almost went over the edge, and I had to cut the lines to save you. Understand? I'm sorry." Iluq had been Kumar's lead dog, close companion, and dear friend. Denali wondered if his father even remembered the dog.

Kumar propped himself up on one elbow and stared at the rift, which spanned several dozen yards across and extended inland as far as eye could see. His expression showed no response to the loss of the dogs.

Denali tried not to let his father's lack of memories bother him. Kumar had hit his head too hard, that was all. He'd get his memories back soon. He had to.

Denali scanned the far side of the fissure for any sign of the tribe but saw nothing but more fissures beyond. It seemed the whole terminal edge of the glacier was breaking apart. He hoped the rest of the tribe had gotten past. His mother had been in the boat, following the shore. If she'd been too close when the edge calved off, the current could have capsized her and pulled her under. Denali swallowed a lump in his throat and forced himself to believe that Eska and the rest of the tribe had passed this way safely.

"I suppose we have to get across or you wouldn't have come back here," Kumar said.

"The rest of the tribe has gone that way, headed for Illulissat. We need to get to them before the snow wolves get to us. We can't fight the wolves alone."

"And when the fissure opened up you went that way?" Kumar pointed inland.

"Yes, there was a blizzard. I couldn't see. The dogs took me past the edge of the fissure to the ice cave. We might be able to hold the wolves off there, but we'd be trapped and probably starve to death. The wolves would just wait until we're too weak to fight them. We need to follow the fissure to the edge and then get the dogs to turn west toward Illulissat. The command to turn left is *Haw*. *Haw*, do you understand? When we get to the end of the fissure, you've got to get the dogs to turn left."

Kumar slumped back against the sled and closed his eyes. "Right."

"Not right. Left."

Kumar snorted. "That's what I meant. Right, I understand you, we have to turn left. *Haw* to go left?"

"Correct." Denali said through gritted teeth.

A chilling howl split the air behind them. The snow wolves had picked up their trail.

Chapter Six

The sled skimmed the surface of snow and ice, hushed by the howling of the wolf pack in the distance. The storm had dropped a thick layer of powder, and then blown it into drifts, so one moment the sled would be running on the ice, the next the dogs would have to forge through a wave of loose snow taller than their heads.

The dogs didn't seem to mind. Instead they made a game of it, picking up as much speed as they could before plowing into the drifts and yipping in delight as the snow burst up in a billow around them.

With the storm gone, Denali could see that his course rose at a slight angle, climbing up toward a cone-shaped mountain in the distance. The ice cave where the Great White dragons had lived was in a fold of the mountain near the base. As Denali rushed toward the mountain, steam rose from the slopes. A huge chunk of ice broke free from the cone near the top and crashed down to form a rumbling avalanche of ice and snow, leaving bare black rock behind.

Denali gripped the handbar so hard his fingers ached inside his mitten. He was a ways from those mountain slopes, but he hand no desire to go up there.

His father lay quiet in the sled, unmoving. The wind whipped Kumar's hood back, and Denali noticed the bump on the back of his head had grown bigger and continued to ooze blood. The smell of blood mixed with the musty scent of the dogs and smell of fish and seaweed that wafted from the bundle on the sled.

The rift gradually narrowed, and Denali was relieved to see the place ahead where the fissure ended. "Father." He reached down and shook Kumar's shoulder.

Kumar moaned and shifted but didn't wake.

Denali shook him harder and shouted, "Father, wake up!" Odds were if his father didn't wake and give the command, the dogs would follow the trail they'd taken the day before, heading right to the mountain with its steaming slopes and avalanches.

Kumar opened his eyes and put his hand to the swelling bump on the back of his head.

The fissure narrowed to a small crack and then vanished. "Haw!" Denali shouted at the dogs.

Two of them tried to turn, but the rest continued forward, dragging the two obedient dogs behind them until they gave up and joined the others.

"No. Haw," Denali gave the command again. The dogs laid their ears back and kept going.

Muttering angrily, Denali threw down the snowhook just as the dogs and sled piled into a deep drift. He tried to stamp the snowhook down, but it wouldn't catch in the loose snow. Curtains of snow shot up on either side of him as the dogs plunged through the drift.

When they came out on the other side, the fissure was a ways behind them.

"Haw," Denali shouted. The dogs let loose a happy howl and rushed toward the next big drift. "Father," Denali reached down and slapped his father's face. "You have to give the command. Please."

"Haw," Kumar muttered.

"Louder." Denali tried to get the snowhook back into a position where he could stamp it into the ice before the next drift.

"Haw!" Kumar shouted.

As one, the five dogs turned and loped westward.

"I really hate those dogs sometimes," Denali muttered. He much preferred to be in his boat where he had complete control of his course as long as he had his paddles. He pulled the snowhook up and hung it back on the side of the sled.

The dogs followed the trough between drifts until it rose to an even level of packed snow across the glacier. Denali kept his eyes open for more rifts. He was relieved to finally be headed westward toward Illulissat, but he'd come inland far enough he could not even see the shoreline. He didn't want to get too close to the calving glacier with all its fissures and crevices, but if he stayed this far inland he might miss Illulissat altogether since it was situated beside a small bay.

"Haw," he told the dogs again.

"Haw," Kumar echoed him. The dogs laid their ears back and turned more to the left, setting their course on a diagonal westward toward shore.

"Thank you," Denali told his father.

"Stupid dogs." Kumar closed his eyes and let out a pained breath.

Denali let the dogs run until their tails hung low and their breath came in labored gasps. Every so often the wolf howls would split the air, but they seemed to be falling farther behind each time they howled. Denali smelled the sea on the wind and heard the waves lapping on the shore before he caught sight of the coast. That was good enough for him. He didn't want to get too close to the shore, just be able to see it.

"Whoa," Denali gave the command to stop. The dogs were tired and agitated about being separated from the rest of the tribe's dogs for so long. The temperature had dropped now that the storm had passed, and Denali longed to crawl into a thick layer of skins and rest. He hadn't slept at all in the cave and knew he couldn't go on forever anymore than the dogs could.

He stared behind him, looking for any movement of the wolves.

The landscape remained empty of any creature other than those with Denali. Far off in the distance, the snow wolves set up a chorus of howls.

Denali shivered and turned back to the sled. His father was awake, but glassy eyed. "The wolves are hunters," Kumar muttered. "I know hunters. They'll fall silent before they attack. As long as we can hear them we should be safe." Denali wasn't sure if his father was trying to reassure himself or Denali.

The dogs doubled back on their lines, sniffed the sled, and pawed at the seal skin that held the food.

"Of course you're hungry," Denali said. "I am too. Back off and give me some room." He shoved Miki and Niki away with his foot and then cut up a couple of dragonfish to give to the dogs. Kumar watched him work, but drew back when Denali held out a chunk of the frozen fish to him.

"Come on, you have to eat," Denali said.

"You expect me to eat raw fish? Frozen, raw fish?" Kumar pushed the food away. "Sorry, no. You eat it."

"But you eat fish every day. It's not as good as seal meat, but still. It's either that or seaweed." Denali peeled a few fronds of seaweed from the bundle and offered them to his father.

Kumar accepted the seaweed, took a bite, and made a face. He puckered his lips as if to spit it out.

"Don't you dare," Denali scolded. "We are close to starving to death. This food is the last, the very last, we're likely to get before we reach Illulissat. And we have to split it between you and me and the dogs. Maybe that bump on your head has made you half crazy, but I won't allow you to waste any more food."

Kumar swallowed the bite he'd taken and nibbled at the rest of the seaweed in his hand. "It's awfully cold," he muttered, "and it seems like it's been night for a very long time. Shouldn't the sun be up by now?"

Denali's gut twisted. He didn't think he could stand much more of his father acting like a Southerner. "No, the sun shouldn't be up," he snapped. "It won't rise for another six weeks. Can you climb off the sled? We need to tip it over to make a windbreak. I don't want to take the time to set up the tent. We'll rest here just for a short while, then get going again, hopefully before the snow wolves catch up to us.

Kumar slid off the sled with a grunt of pain and waited in the snow while Denali unpacked the sled and tipped it up on its side. The dogs settled down into fuzzy balls as Denali stretched the tent hides over the sled and down to the ground, forming a narrow shelter.

Inside, he made a bed by spreading the remaining furs out on the ground and using the bundle of Kumar's personal items as a pillow. He urged his father into the shelter then crawled in after, lying down with one hand on spear and the other on his father's hunting knife. The tent muffled the wolf howls, but the sound of so many terrified Denali. At least if he could hear them, he'd know where they were.

He woke to a sudden silence. Straining his ears, all he could hear was the sound of his father's soft breathing and the wind rushing across the ice and snow. Still gripping the spear and hunting knife, he crawled out of the shelter and looked around.

The wind had blown a thin layer of snow over the sleeping dogs, making them look like a cluster of snow mounds. Denali turned in a circle, searching the ice and snow drifts for the wolves. Cold fingers of fear raced up and down his spine. As hard as he looked, he could not make out the wolves. Their pelts matched the landscape, and in the half-light, the only chance Denali had of recognizing them was if they moved. Kapik had told him once that a snow wolf could hold still for hours, waiting for its prey.

Denali shuddered and whistled the dogs awake. They popped out of the snow and milled around in a tight knot, waiting for breakfast. He cut up the rest of the fish and tossed the first chunk to the closest dog.

A pearl-escent head snaked above the dogs and snatched the fish from the air before it reached its intended recipient.

The hatchling white dragon swallowed the fish without even bothering to chew.

"Hey," Denali shouted in surprise. He hadn't noticed the little dragon there until its head shot up. "That wasn't for you. You already stole more than your share of fish."

The dogs whined for their food, looking up expectantly at Denali.

The baby dragon sat and mewled up at him like the rest of the dogs. With its big blue eyes looking at Denali, he could almost feel the dragon's hunger. He tossed it his own piece of fish, then gave each of the dogs its share straight from his hand so the dragon couldn't steal it.

The hatchling pressed up against him and rubbed its head on Denali's legs. An overwhelming feeling of loneliness washed over him.

"Well, that's a pretty sight." Kumar's deep voice made Denali jump and sent the little dragon scampering back among the dogs.

Denali turned to see that Kumar had pulled himself out from beneath the shelter. The back of his head was still bleeding and swollen even more than it had been before. Kumar grabbed the sled and hauled himself to his feet. He wavered and would have fallen if he hadn't been holding onto the sled for support.

"I don't know how she got here," Denali said. "I never saw her following us."

Kumar frowned. "She seems to like you."

"It's not my fault," Denali said. "I attacked her in the cave. Cut her. It doesn't make any sense that she would have followed me."

Kumar squinted across the horizon. "The howls have stopped."

"I know. We need to leave quickly. But what about the dragon?"

"You gave her your fish." Kumar's voice was sharp. "After you insisted we'd starve if we wasted anything."

Denali turned away from his father and began taking down the shelter and packing their things. "She felt so hungry it made me hurt. I can eat seaweed. She can't."

"You *felt* her hunger?" Kumar pushed the sled back down flat on its runners. It landed with a loud thump that made Denali twitch.

Denali knew what he'd said sounded crazy. It didn't make sense even to him. He didn't dare admit he'd also felt how lonely the hatchling was. Its parents were dead, and it just wanted to be with Denali. Its pleading eyes made his chest hurt with longing.

Kumar wobbled and slumped onto the sled. Denali packed everything around him.

Kumar grabbed his arm in a tight grip. "Did you or did you not *feel* the dragon's hunger."

Denali pulled away and climbed onto the back of the sled. "It doesn't matter. We have to get out of here. We'll go westward, staying parallel with the shore. Tell the dogs to get moving."

"It does matter," Kumar said. "It matters a lot. Your life could be in danger."

"Of course my life is in danger; we're being hunted by snow w—"

A giant wolf leaped from behind Denali. It landed beside the dogs, tore Niki out of his harness, and bounded away between one breath and the next. Denali hurled the spear at the wolf, but only grazed its rump.

"Don't throw the spear," Kumar said too late.

A second wolf leaped from its hiding place in a snowdrift behind the sled. It landed on top of Denali, flattening him against the ground. Its sharp jaws snapped toward Denali's neck.

Chapter Seven

Kumar shouted and jumped on the wolf's back. The wolf was twice as big as Denali, but Kumar wrapped a muscled arm around the wolf's neck and pulled its snapping jaws away.

The wolf twisted its head and tried to bite Kumar's face. Kumar adjusted his hold and squeezed, cutting off the wolf's breath.

"Give me the knife," Kumar said through gritted teeth. He flailed with his free hand, trying to reach the hunting knife that was pinned in Denali's hand.

The wolf's claws pawed at Denali's shoulders and chest as it struggled to dislodge Kumar.

Denali cried out and shifted his hand to leave part of the hilt free, then he thrashed until he broke loose enough to press the hunting knife into Kumar's hand.

As soon as Kumar got hold of the knife, he sliced the blade across wolf's throat. The wolf struggled for another moment while its life slipped away.

Kumar pushed it off Denali, and it slumped down dead in the snow. Kumar rolled to one knee with his splinted leg stretched out beside him, the hunting knife ready for another attack.

"Get the spear," he told Denali.

Denali jumped to his feet, heart racing, fear sour on his tongue. His jacket was torn, but the claws had only scratched his skin a little. He ran to the spear, picked it up, and looked around. Nothing moved except the dogs, who whined and pressed close together. The little white dragon huddled in their midst.

Kumar got on the sled and motioned Denali to come. Denali ran back, pulled the snowhook free, and yelled at the dogs to get moving.

The dogs hesitated, looking around in fear.

"Hike!" Kumar yelled.

The team snapped into motion.

"Haw," Kumar guided the dogs to the left to run parallel with the shore. The white dragon flapped into the air and settled itself onto the sled at Kumar's feet.

Denali leaned over the handbar, sick with fear. "I'm sorry I threw the spear. I thought if I could hit the wolf I could save Niki."

He glanced behind, wondering where the rest of the wolf pack was. He had the spear in his hand now and wouldn't make the mistake of letting it go again.

"The dog was already dead. Its neck snapped when the wolf tore it from the harness." Kumar slumped back and put a hand to his head, but he kept the hunting knife ready in his other hand. "Those are really big wolves," he muttered.

An excited howl split the air behind them. Denali looked back in time to see a half-dozen wolves tear into the carcass of the dead one, feasting with sickening slurps and crunches.

"Hike," Denali yelled at the dogs. They picked up speed. He hoped the wolves behind him would eat their fill from their fallen pack member and let Denali go.

"You all right?" Kumar asked.

"I'm fine." Denali was shaken but not hurt too bad.

The sled went over a bump, and the hatchling dragon dug its claws into Kumar's legs to keep from being tossed off the sled.

"Ouch." Kumar kicked the dragon with his good leg.

The hatchling flapped up and landed square on Kumar's chest. Its long tongue flicked out and licked the swollen back of Kumar's head. Kumar grunted in annoyance and let the dragon lick the wound. When it had finished, it curled up on Kumar's chest and gazed at Denali with its big eyes. Its dragonstone glowed softly in contentment. It hoped Denali would let it stay with him if it tried to be useful.

Denali reached a hand out and stroked the dragon's sleek face. She was so beautiful. So delicate, like frost crystals on frozen water. "All right, Frost. You can stay," Denali said. Frost sounded like the perfect name for the baby white dragon.

Frost let out a happy purring sound.

"Not on my chest you can't." Kumar shoved the baby dragon off his chest and scooted over to the side so they'd both fit on the sled.

"This is the craziest thing I've ever done," he muttered. "Who'd have thought the greatest dragon hunter alive would ride side-by-side with a dragon hatchling." He shook his head in disgust. Frost licked his face.

"I think she likes you," Denali said.

Kumar grimaced. "I have a feeling that's not the whole pack back there?"

Denali shook his head. "It would be an awfully small one if it was."

"Then we can expect more trouble." Kumar leaned back and closed his eyes. His face was too pale. The fight with the wolf had taken all the strength he had left.

"Let's hope not," Denali whispered. But he knew his father was right. They still had a long way to go to reach Illulissat. The rest of the tribe had left them far behind and had probably already arrived.

ORAGONBOUNO

Shivering, Kanvar tried to undo the straps that held him to Dharanidhar's neck, but his hands were too numb to work the clasps very well. He couldn't stop shaking, and the cold just kept getting colder. He worked himself loose finally and slid to the rocky ground, but his frozen feet and legs refused to hold him for a moment.

Dhar caught him before he fell on his face. *I'd fly you right into the center of town if I could, but I'm sure the humans wouldn't take it well. Can you walk?*

"Of course I can walk. I just need a moment to get my blood flowing again." Kanvar rubbed at his stumpy arm and shook out his legs. He and Dharanidhar had reached a moon-shaped bay and taken refuge in a sea cave out by the headland. The Varnan colony of Illulissat spread in a disordered jumble of houses beside the bay. Chunks of ice floated in the water, and a thick layer of snow draped the buildings in white.

I don't know, Dhar grumbled. *I think I better fly you a bit closer. The ground looks pretty slippery.*

"You worry too much, Dhar." Kanvar checked to make sure his crossbow and bolts were still secure on his back and his hunting knife in the sheath at his waist.

"A bit of a walk is just what I need to get my blood flowing again. I'll buy some warmer clothes as soon as I get into town."

Do you have enough money?

Kanvar pressed his hand against the bag of coins he wore tucked under his jacket on a leather thong around his neck. He laughed. No matter how many times Kanvar had explained the value of each of the coins, Dhar never seemed to catch on to what the little round gold things were really worth. Lucky for Kanvar, Dhar had taken the pretty things back to his cave whenever he'd come across them. "It's plenty. Believe me."

Kanvar took a deep breath and limped to the cave opening. The tide had just gone out, leaving a swath of black pebbles he could follow around to the colony. Better that than trying to cross the snowy patches further up on shore.

Behind him, Dhar settled to the ground and folded his wings up against his sides. *I'm hungry,* he grumbled. *Why do you suppose all those extra little fat critters were on the coast of Kundiland instead of here where they belong? What I wouldn't give for just a few more tasty sea lions.*

Kanvar tucked his hands under his jacket and hurried as fast as he could, which was never very fast, toward Illulissat. At least it wasn't as cold on the ground as it had been in the air with the frozen wind tearing his breath away. Normally he loved flying with Dharanidhar, but the farther north they'd come, the more excruciating the experience had been.

Illulissat was the strangest town Kanvar had ever seen. When he'd lived in Daro the streets were narrow and straight, lined with tall mud-brick buildings. At the Maran Colony, the streets had been much wider. The colony buildings had been mostly one story, but made of black volcanic rock to withstand dragon fire from the attacking Great Blue dragons.

But Illulissat wasn't like the Maran Colony or Daro. The houses were single, unconnected structures, thrown up here and there in random places with a maze of twisted paths between them.

The wooden houses had steep roofs, and the other houses—Kanvar thought they might be houses, but he wasn't sure—looked like someone had cut up big blocks of grassy earth and stacked them up, slapped on a front door and a window here and there, and covered the top with more earth, ice, and snow.

Kanvar figured living there must be like living in a hole in the ground. Dark gray smoke lifted from the top of chimneys, smelling like burning fish oil. In fact, the whole town smelled like dead and decaying fish.

Despite the floating chunks of ice, a Varnan merchant ship sat in the bay, its sails furled, its decks quiet.

Dozens of small boats made with whalebone frames and covered with animal hides, crowded around the wooden docks.

People wrapped in heavy fur clothing moved about slowly as if they'd never dreamed of the rush and hurry of people in Daro's busy streets or the labor-intensive life of the Maran Colony in Kundiland.

As Kanvar approached the docks, a dozen more boats paddled to shore. The docks were all full, so the occupants hopped out on the rocks then lifted the boats, which seemed to be packed with skins and personal belonging, and carried them up onto the snow.

At the same time, a chorus of howls filled the air. A pack of dogs appeared on the rise above the town and loped toward shore. They pulled some sort of a sled behind them where several people sat, urging the dogs on. The first team of dogs was followed by another and another until the air rang with howls and shouts of people as the whole group came in.

Breathing hard, Kanvar limped away from the water toward what he hoped was the center of town. As he left the rocks behind, he stepped onto snow, lost his footing and fell. The cold ice stung his hand as he tried to get back up.

His good leg slipped again, and he went face-first back into the snow. A pair of Varnan fishermen laughed at him from the dock.

Kanvar rolled to a sit and glared at them. He'd never had to walk on snow and ice before. Dhar was right, the ground was slippery. Kanvar felt like he had when he'd been young and it had taken him so much longer to learn to walk than other children. Years longer, but it hadn't stopped him from trying. And it wouldn't stop him now.

He got up again, took two steps, and thumped back down flat on his rear.

The Varnans laughed harder. "Poor little crippled boy. Go back to Daro. Illulissat is only for real men."

Ignoring them, Kanvar got back up. The problem was his twisted left leg would not steady him enough to move his right leg forward without slipping. Perhaps if he took smaller steps. He tried that method, but fell again for a fourth time.

As Kanvar was picking himself up yet again, the first team of dogs reached the shore. The men on the sled hopped off and were greeted by the people who had just landed in the boats.

DRAGONBOUND

One of the men unstrapped a whale bone spear from the sled and strode across the ice and snow to Kanvar. His thick fur clothes concealed his whole body except for a wrinkled face that peered out from a crack in the hood.

"Southerners." The man spit in the direction of the Varnans, flipped the spear over so it was point down, and held it out to Kanvar.

The Varnan fishermen snorted and walked away.

Kanvar took the spear in his numb hand and used it to steady himself on the slippery ground.

"You come on the boat?" The old man pointed to the Varnan ship in the bay. His accent was so thick, Kanvar might not have understood him if he hadn't picked up the flicker of thought from the old man's mind.

Kanvar nodded. Well, he couldn't admit he'd flown in on a Great Blue dragon, could he?

"You can't go around dressed like that here." The old man's voice was gruff but kind.

"I know." Kanvar's teeth chattered. He hadn't been warm for a couple of days. "I-I just need to buy some warm clothes. Could you . . . if you could just point out the closest store."

"Nah, you don't want a Southerner store. They don't know how to dress either. You need real clothes. Come with me." The old man turned back toward the edge of town where most of the dog teams had stopped and people had set about constructing some kind of shelters made from whale bones and skins.

Using the spear to steady himself, Kanvar limped after the old man. "What's your name?" he asked as he struggled to keep up.

"Kapik," the old man called back. He reached a gray-hared woman who was working on a shelter, put his arm around her shoulders, and whispered something to her. She looked over at Kanvar.

Kanvar stopped moving. People always stared at him for an uncomfortable amount of time when they first saw him. It took that long for someone to wrap their mind around his twisted left leg and stumpy right arm with its withered two fingers and thumb that served for a hand.

Finally she looked away, muttered something unintelligible to Kapik, and went to a bundle still tied to the sledge. Kanvar could tell from her thoughts that she was Kapik's wife, and he had asked if they had clothes that might fit Kanvar. She didn't seem to think so, since no one Kanvar's age shared their tent anymore. And she knew full well that no jacket that anyone in the tribe had would fit Kanvar's left arm. She'd have to sew something especially for him. That would take a while, and Kanvar would freeze to death long before she finished.

Several men from the tribe gathered around Kapik. They were agitated. Upset. Hungry. Yes, hungry. Kanvar picked up the overwhelming need for food from everyone around him. They'd come to Illulissat, hoping the Southerners would have food to spare, but the tribe had very little it could give in trade for the food. Kanvar shook his head and built a shield to protect his mind from their hunger. It was bad enough with Dharanidhar's stomach grumbling in the back of his thoughts.

"Atka, how are your eyes?" Kapik asked one of the other men.

Atka blinked and rubbed his eyes. "Better, I can see light and shadow now instead of just blackness."

"Good. Let's hope for a complete recovery." Kapik slapped Atka's shoulder and then went back over to his wife. "Did you find anything, Desna?"

Desna shook her head, muttered some more, and went over to a younger woman who sat alone on a pile of belongings she'd carried up from one of the boats. She had her head buried in her hands and made no move to construct a shelter like the rest of the people were doing. Her shoulders shook, and Kanvar realized she was crying. Her grief threatened to drown him. He cut his mind off completely from all of these people and took a step back.

A big man with sharp eyes noticed Kanvar flinch away. He sneered at Kanvar. "That's right Southerner. Get lost. Your people are nothing but trouble. We always had plenty to eat before you came here."

"Tartok, leave the boy alone," Kapik snapped.

Two other men grabbed Tartok and dragged him away. "Be quiet," they admonished when they thought they were out of earshot. "We need his money to buy food. You should be grateful Kapik has found someone to sell furs to already. We might just eat tonight if you don't ruin it."

Kanvar pressed his hand against the money pouch beneath his jacket and wondered how much it would take to feed so many people.

He walked over to where Kapik was busy staking out his dogs and taking off their harnesses. "Are-are you the Tuniit Tribe?" Kanvar didn't know how many tribes existed in the Great North. Several at least he guessed from the number of boats that had been at the docks before the newcomers had arrived.

Kapik stopped with a dog's foreleg halfway out of the harness and looked over at Kanvar. His eyebrows pressed together. "Possibly. Say it again?"

Feeling foolish, Kanvar repeated himself. "The Tuniit Tribe?"

Kapik looked back to the dog and finished slipping the harness off before answering. "Yes. I think that's how you Southerners pronounce it. We say Tuniit though." The way Kapik said the name it sounded almost like a different word.

Kanvar mimicked the pronunciation.

"That's closer," Kapik said. "But how do you know of us?"

Desna rushed over before Kanvar had a chance to answer. She carried a thick hooded coat that had two layers of furs sewn together: a soft gray lining of fur on the inside, and a sparkling layer of silver fur on the outside. She wrapped it around Kanvar and it extended down just below his knees. Clucking over him, she shoved a matching mitten onto his right hand and tucked its mate into a pocket. Then she held out a pair of thick fur boots.

"Put them on," she said. Since Kanvar had locked out all the Tuniits' thoughts, he couldn't tell exactly what she had said, because of her thick accent, but he understood her intent.

He eased himself to the ground, took of his dragonhide boots, and pulled on the replacements.

Bundled in the new clothes, Kanvar felt heat returning to his body. He took the coat off long enough to unstrap his crossbow harness, then slipped back into the coat and reattached the harness on the outside. He had to loosen the straps to their fullest length to make up for the new coat's excess bulk.

Desna pulled Kapik aside and started whispering to him. Kanvar lowered the shields around his mind a bit to catch what she said.

"It's Denali's long-coat. She made it as a surprise for his twelfth birthday. Kapik, I think she will die of a broken heart seeing some other boy wear it. And it's too small for this Southerner really. Tell him it's just temporary. He must give it back as soon as I make something for him. Please, Kapik. This is one thing too much for Eska right now."

"Desna." Kapik squeezed his wife's shoulders. "You know Denali is dead. She has no use for the coat."

"No." Desna poked Kapik in the chest with a mittened hand. "Don't talk like that. He's alive. I know it. Kumar said he'd meet us here, and he'll do it. You wait and see. He's a strong man and he won't let any harm come to Denali."

Kapik shook his head. "They're dead, Desna. No one could survive that dragon. And if they had escaped it somehow, they would have caught up to us by now. We waited long enough for them. They didn't come, because they can't come. The dragon froze them solid, and all your hoping won't change that fact and it won't help Eska come to terms with their deaths."

Desna swore, pushed Kapik away, and stalked back over to the grieving Eska.

Kanvar sat in the snow, holding his dragonskin boots. The new coat had warmed him for a moment, but Kapik and Desna's argument had frozen him to the core. He couldn't move. He couldn't think. He'd tried so hard to get here in time to save his grandfather.

Chapter Eight

Kanvar sat stunned for a few moments, watching the Tuniits set up their camp, unable to believe he'd come too late to save his grandfather.

Get up, Dharanidhar spoke into his mind. *We don't know if we're too late or not. The woman doesn't think so. Your grandfather might have defeated the Great White dragon.*

Kanvar couldn't picture how his grandfather would have survived a confrontation with the Great White.

Without his armor? Without his weapons? Unable to remember any of his training?

REBECCA SHELLEY

We don't know exactly what he does or doesn't remember, Dhar said. *And judging from how helpful your armor hasn't been up here, he was probably better off dressed as a Tuniit. Your armor is made to resist poison and fire, not cold. Now get up and come back to the cave.*

Kanvar tucked his dragonhide boots into the front of his coat, then used the spear to leverage himself to his feet and limp over to Eska who still sat with Desna's arm wrapped around her.

Kanvar untied the pouch of money from his neck and pulled it out from beneath his long-coat.

"Eska?" he said.

She looked up at him and shuddered, but didn't say anything.

Kanvar leaned over and pressed the money pouch into her hand. "My name is Kanvar. I'm Kumar's grandson. I had a nightmare that he faced a Great White dragon, and I've come to save him. He's fought a lot of dragons in his lifetime. I don't think he's dead. I'm going to go look for him and Denali and bring them back to you." Kanvar hobbled away without waiting for a response from the Tuniit woman.

He left Kapik's spear at the edge of the snow patch and hurried back to Dharanidhar.

DRAGONBOUND

Denali gripped the spear while the dogs ran over the glacier's rough ice. Snow from the recent storm had filled in most of the cracks, making the sled's passage possible. Ahead a giant snow drift barred the way, promising a difficult slog up over it.

Denali gritted his teeth and looked behind him. The wolves had fallen silent again.

"I don't like it," he told Frost.

Frost burbled in reply.

"Too bad I can't understand what you're saying." Denali could feel the dragon's emotions, but she didn't talk to him the way a human would.

His father lay unconscious on the sled. His face pale, his head swollen.

The dogs reached the steep slope of the drift and slowed as they punched through the soft snow up to their chests. Denali jumped from the back of the sled and ran behind, pushing it to help the dogs. He was down to four dogs, and his father wasn't a small man. Panting, the dogs stopped halfway up to catch their breath. Denali leaned against the handbar. His muscles burned from the exertion. His stomach grumbled, complaining that he'd fed everyone but himself.

A tuft of snow puffed up at the top of the drift, caught on the wind, and was swept away.

Denali stiffened and looked up. Another puff of snow kicked up, and then a dozen wolves topped the rise and lunged down toward him.

"Hike," Denali screamed. "Gee." He pushed the sled into motion and jumped on the runners as the startled dogs bolted to the right, tearing the sled across the edge of the drift and then back down onto flat ground, heading inland toward the steaming mountain. The terrified dogs ran flat out, but the giant wolves kept pace a few yards off to his left with long easy strides.

Denali gripped the handbar with his left hand and lifted the spear, readying for an attack. But the main body of wolves stayed parallel with him while three others fell back and came up at his rear.

"Gee," Denali cried again, urging the dogs further to the right, trying to set the sled on course for the white dragons' cave. It was a long way, but he had to do something. "Father, wake up!" he shouted.

Kumar did not respond.

Off to Denali's right, movements on the ice caught his attention. The wolves he'd encountered before sped toward him, blocking any escape to the east.

Denali's pounding heart sounded louder than the pad of the dogs' feet on the ice and the creak of the lead lines straining to pull the sled. A cold wind sliced his cheeks. Gradually the two sets of wolves drew closer, pinning him between them, forcing the dogs straight ahead.

A hundred fears tumbled through Denali's mind. He was trapped. He knew it. The wolves knew it. They were playing with him. Letting him run, knowing he would not escape. The snow wolves would hunt a giant ice bear this way, and Denali was no threat compared to that.

"They're going to eat us, Frost," Denali said. "I'll be lucky to kill one of them before they do." He counted almost twenty.

Frost reared up on her hind legs, spread her wings, and hissed. The sled jolted. She lost her balanced and thumped back down beside Kumar.

Denali let out a grim chuckle. "Yes, you are ferocious little girl. I'm sure that will scare them all away."

Frost lowered her head and whined.

The dogs slowed, winded from their fast sprint and the weight of the sled.

The wolves slowed as well, matching their pace with Denali's and pressing close enough to the sled that Denali could see their silver eyes and saliva dripping from their open jaws. He shivered with fear. The wolf pack was ten times more terrifying than the Great White dragon had been. But then Denali had not had time to be truly frightened of the dragon. The battle with it had happened so fast.

The wolves were in no hurry. They enjoyed running their prey to a standstill.

One of the wolves behind Denali lunged forward and snapped at his legs. Denali swung the haft of the spear and hit the wolf in the face.

It snarled and fell back.

"Hike," Denali shouted at the dogs. They made a halfhearted attempt to redouble their speed, but soon fell back to a trot. Foam frothed at the edges of their mouths from the effort, and they rolled their eyes in terror, looking from the wolves on one side of them, to the wolves closing in on the other. The ground rose into a slope, slowing the dogs even more.

"Father!" Denali tried to shake Kumar awake. While Denali was bent over, the wolf behind him snapped at his legs again. Its sharp teeth tore through his thick seal-skin pants and grazed his calves.

Denali screamed and hit at the wolf. This time it dodged his blow.

Frost hissed and blew a puff of cold air into Kumar's face, then licked his cheeks. Kumar opened bleary eyes and stared up at Denali.

"The wolves," Denali shouted. "They're upon us."

Kumar pulled himself up to a sit and gazed groggily around. His eyes widened, and the hand holding the hunting knife jerked up into a defensive position. "What are they waiting for?" he muttered.

The sled topped a rise and then slewed down into a narrow valley between two arms of the mountain. A sheer cliff of ice blocked their path straight ahead. Denali stared up at it in horror. The wolves had run him straight into a trap, pinning him against the cliff face.

The dogs stopped and turned to face the closing circle of wolves. The sled slid down beside them and bumped up against the cliff. Denali jumped off, put his back to the ice, and readied the spear. The wolves stalked forward. Denali's head barely reached to their shoulders.

Kumar forced himself up to stand beside Denali. The dogs whimpered and cowered back against the cliff. Kumar cut their lines so they could run, though Denali doubted any of them would escape the hungry wolves.

Frost jumped from the sled and rubbed against Denali's leg as the wolves inched closer, growling and snapping.

"Get behind me," Denali told Frost. "Stay out of the way." He hoped the wolves would leave the baby dragon alone. If they were smart, they'd know she would turn to ice in their mouths if they killed her. Great White dragons, even baby ones, were not edible prey.

Frost stayed beside Denali, hissing and spreading her wings the way her father had when he confronted Kumar. Though Denali figured the little dragon would be little help against the wolves, he suddenly felt better having her beside him, like she was trying to reassure him that everything would be all right.

"I don't think so, Frost," Denali said.

"Is that dragon talking to you?" Kumar asked.

The closest wolf lunged at him, snapping at his arm. Kumar twisted his knife hand out of the way at the last moment and sliced the wolf across the eyes.

It howled and fell back.

"What can it hurt? We're going to die anyway," Denali said.

Two wolves lunged at him. He thrust the spear into the one on the right.

"I don't intend to die," Kumar grunted as he threw himself at the second wolf, slitting its throat.

The wolf Denali had speared, twisted away and leaped back, tearing the spear out of Denali's hands.

Kumar swore, rolled up to his good knee and grabbed the haft of the spear as it swung past him. He tore the spear from the chest of the retreating wolf and used it to get to his feet, then held it out to Denali.

Denali shook his head. "You should keep it. I'm no good with it. I'm too little." Denali was shaking and couldn't stop. His father had blinded one wolf already and killed another.

Denali's spear thrust had injured the third wolf but not killed it instantly. He'd missed its heart.

"Take it," Kumar shouted at him. "I can't fight them alone. I need you. Just let the next one get a little bit closer before you strike, and keep a better grip on the haft. Take your mittens off. They're too slippery."

Denali pulled the mittens off. The cold wind bit at his hands. The wolves' growls deepened, and the main body of them closed in.

He took the spear back from his father.

Kumar steadied himself with one hand against the cliff and breathed deeply, eyes focused on the wolves, waiting for the next one to move.

Denali lifted the spear, but couldn't decide which of the wolves to point it toward. He jerked it back and forth unsure of where to strike.

"Steady there," Kumar said. "They can't all come at once. They don't have enough room. Watch their front shoulders. They'll crouch in preparation to leap. Probably two or three at a time. If we stay back-to-back up against the cliff, they won't be able to come around behind us. We'll only have to take a few of them at a time."

Kumar sounded so sure of what the wolves would do. He seemed to know, like somehow he knew the Great White dragon would flash its stone before attacking. "How do you know?" Denali asked. "Have you fought the snow wolves before?"

Three wolves lunged forward, but not at Denali and Kumar. They went for the dogs, tearing into them. The dogs tried to run, but only Miki got away, streaking across the snow as fast as he could, his tail tight between his legs. Denali half-hoped he would get clean away and half-hoped some of the other wolves would go chase him down, leaving less to attack Denali. But with the dogs out of the way, all the wolves turned their full attention on Kumar and Denali.

"No. I haven't fought snow wolves before," Kumar said in a choked voice. Perhaps he finally remembered how much he'd loved his dogs. "But I've faced other predators. At least these boys don't breathe fire or spit acid. After you've faced down a Great Red dragon in its lair, what's a little pack of snow wolves?" He let out a bitter laugh that did not reassure Denali.

Chapter Nine

Dharanidhar flew low across the snowy ground so that Kanvar could see the path the Tuniits' sleds had left in the snow. If they'd fled from the Great White dragon leaving Kumar to fight it, than their tracks should lead back there.

To the right, waves hissed against hot black rocks, sending up showers of steam. A bit further out, the water gurgled over a bright red-orange glow, and a geyser shot into the air higher than Dharanidhar.

Dhar pulled up and glided inland. *I don't think following that trail is safe*, he told Kanvar.

The steaming water made Kanvar nervous, but didn't seem dangerous. He was warmer now, though the long-coat was a tight fit on him, obviously meant for a smaller boy. "If we don't stay close, we could lose the trail. What are you afraid of? A little steam won't hurt you." Great Blue dragons breathed the hottest fire on the planet. Their thick scales kept them safe from any heat or cold.

That was boiling hot water, Kanvar. It was high enough to blow right into your face. Ignoring what it might do to your skin, just think what would happen to us if it burned your eyes.

Kanvar shuddered. "Just stay as close as you can. I'm having trouble seeing it in the dark. I wonder if it ever gets light here."

Probably not. Dhar snorted and edged back over to fly above the trail. *Your father picked the most miserable out-of-the-way place in the whole world to send your grandfather, and Amar prides himself on being such a nice guy.*

Kanvar couldn't argue with that. He wondered why anyone would want to live here, and how they survived if they did.

A little while later, the tracks they'd been following ended at a site where the snow had been trampled down in a wide circle.

"Looks like the tribe camped here," Kanvar said. "But there are no sled tracks leading up to the campsite, just the ones we've been following that left it."

Dhar landed and sniffed the snow all around the edge of the site. *They came in from the east, still following the shoreline. But there must have been a big snowstorm, because the tracks are all covered.* He leaped back into the air and continued eastward, but the path led out onto a glacier, rife with cracks and fissures.

"I don't know how they could have crossed here," Kanvar said. A thunderous cracking sound filled the air, and a giant chunk of ice broke off from the glacier and splashed down into the frothy waves.

Kanvar gasped at the wondrous beauty and terrifying power of the falling ice.

It must not have been like this before the snowstorm, Dhar said. *It's the only thing that makes sense. Water, ice, snow, these things can change the landscape quickly.* He kept flying in a straight line, but a few wing flaps farther they came to a giant rift in the ice. It spread so wide that Kanvar could hardly see to the other side in the dark. A horrible churning growl came from water rushing along deep in the crevice.

Dhar rose in the air and circled above the divide. *Not a good sign,* he rumbled. *This had to have opened up after the tribe passed this way.*

"That would explain why Kumar and Denali hadn't caught up with them." Kanvar's gut twisted. There had only been the Great White dragon in his dreams, not blizzards, boiling water, geysers, and giant cracks in the ground. His grandfather wouldn't have survived a fall into that crevice.

I thought we agreed that Kumar is still alive, and we will find him, Dhar said, sensing Kanvar's renewed doubt.

"I don't know," Kanvar said, gripping the leather straps that held him on Dhar's neck. "I just don't know."

Well I do, and I intend to keep on looking. Dhar swept back close to the ground on the far side of the rift so Kanvar could try to pick up the trail. As Dhar brought him closer to the ground, Kanvar saw a single set of sled tracks in the snow. It came up to the rift, then turned and ran alongside it.

"There," Kanvar shouted. "More sled tracks. He is alive."

Dhar turned inland where the dark silhouette of a cone-shaped mountain hung against the horizon, smoke billowing from its top.

Ɔenali's frozen fingers shook on the spear. The snow wolves' heads rose above him. Their silver eyes looked down at their prey. Saliva dripped from their sharp teeth and froze as it fell to the ground. The wolves advanced, shoulder to shoulder, their mottled white fur forming an inescapable wall. Their frosty breath smelled like rotten flesh and made Denali's stomach churn.

Denali bit his lip so hard, the coppery taste of blood seeped across his tongue.

A deep growling rose from the wolves' throats. The mountain growled back in answer, and the ground shook.

Denali spread his feet wider to keep his balance on the unstable ground.

With his broken leg, Kumar could not adjust for the unexpected movement. The quaking knocked him off his feet, and the wolves lunged.

Denali waited until the wolf that came at him was right on top of him, then he thrust the spear into the wolf's chest.

The wolf's jaws snapped closed an inch from Denali's face, and the wolf twisted away.

This time, Denali was ready for it. He gripped the spear with both hands and tore it free from the wolf just in time to stab it into the next one. But the next wolf's weight against the spear forced him to the ground. The wolf landed on top of him with the spear in its heart.

Frost let out a high-pitched scream that shattered bits of ice off the cliff. A white light flashed so bright, Denali could see the bones through the skin and muscle of the wolf on top of him. Fortunately the wolf's body had blocked his eyes from the full impact of the light.

A sharp crackling sound filled the air.

Denali crawled out from under the wolf and pulled his spear free. He found Frost right beside him, and a wolf with its jaws ready to close on her. The impact would have snapped Frost's neck, but the wolf was frozen in its position, encased in ice.

Frost ducked under the wolf's stomach and flapped over to Kumar. When he'd fallen, the wolves had grabbed him by the arms and legs and dragged him away from the cliff. One wolf lay dead with the hunting knife in its chest, but Kumar's arms and legs had been savaged by the other wolves.

He lay unmoving, face-first in the snow.

Frost's light flash had blinded several of the wolves and startled the whole pack into retreating a few yards. But they had not run far. They growled with renewed fury. They could smell blood and knew their prey was right in front of them, even though some of them could not longer see it.

Denali rushed to his father and rolled him over. His eyes were closed, his face blue. Denali felt for a pulse and found only the faintest flutter of a heartbeat. Just the slightest wisp of frosty air escaped from between Kumar's lips.

Denali's heart turned to ice. His father had fallen unconscious and left Denali to face the wolf pack alone.

Frost let out a keening wail and licked at the wolf bites on Kumar's arms and legs.

The remaining wolves circled.

Denali had moved away from the cliff and had nothing to protect his back. He gripped his spear and turned with the wolves, trying to see all around him at the same time. They had him now, and they knew it. They licked their lips and pressed closer.

A wave of sudden anger from the baby dragon blasted away Denali's fear.

Frost rose on her hind legs, spread her wings, and positioned herself back-to-back with him. A strong impression came to Denali's mind that seemed to say, *You are not alone.*

Frost's anger gave him courage. He set his spear and waited for the next attack.

It came all too quickly. Five wolves leaped forward at once; three at Frost, one in front of her and one to each side; two at Denali, coming from both left and right at the same time.

Eyes, a snap impression came from Frost.

Denali squeezed his eyes closed and swung the spear in an arc, trying to ward off both of his attackers at once.

Frost flashed and breathed a burst of frozen air at the wolf to her left at the same time she leaped into the air, caught hold of Denali's shoulders, and lifted him above the wolves' heads.

A crackling sound filled the air as one wolf froze.

The two unfrozen wolves, which Frost had blinded, tore into the wolves that had meant to attack Denali, and the four wolves started fighting each other.

But Frost wasn't strong enough to hold Denali off the ground for more than a second. She dropped him, and he landed face-to-face with the biggest wolf of the pack. A giant silver monster that knocked Denali to the ground next to the wolf Kumar had killed and tried to tear Denali's throat out.

Denali blocked its open jaws with the haft of the spear, straining to keep the wolf's head away from him.

The silver wolf snapped its mouth closed, shattering the spear's whale-bone haft.

Denali dropped the spear, grabbed the hunting knife from the chest of the dead wolf, and slashed it across the silver wolf's throat.

Blood sprayed in Denali's face, but he rolled to his feet and turned to face two more attackers.

Eyes, Frost warned him.

Denali closed his eyes and slashed at the noses of the wolves in front of him.

A satisfying crackling sound filled the air as Frost froze another wolf.

Denali opened his eyes and dove between the two wolves in front of him, raking the hunting knife down the side of one of the wolves as he went.

Feeling the cut of the knife, that wolf turned ferocious jaws onto its neighbor.

Denali rolled to his feet behind them and turned, looking for his next opponent.

The snow in front of the cliffs was littered with wolf bodies and frozen wolf statues. Five wolves remained. Two of them blind, three of them unhurt, all of them devilishly angry. They shied away from Frost and made a combined rush at Denali from all sides.

Fear no longer bothered Denali, it had been replaced by an unwavering determination to move and fight and stay alive.

The mountain grumbled, and the ground shook again, harder than before.

Ignoring the shaking ground, the wolves converged on Denali. He rushed at the one in front of him. At the last moment, he dove to the ground, slid across the ice between the wolf's feet, and slashed the hunting knife the full length of its belly. The wolf crumpled to the ground.

The remaining four wolves met where Denali had been standing. They twisted and bounded after him.

Denali jumped to his feet and turned to face them. Frost was behind him. She leaped into the air and flapped toward him, but he could tell she wouldn't reach his side before the last four wolves came down on him.

Duck.

Denali threw himself to the ground and covered his eyes. Light flashed, and a crackling sound filled the air.

When Denali moved his arm away from his face and looked up, he found the four wolves frozen to ice right above him. He crawled out from under their feet and stood. Frost flapped to the ground and wrapped a wing around his legs. He rubbed her smooth head, and her dragonstone warmed his bare fingers.

"I don't believe it," Denali said, looking out across the battlefield. Nothing moved except for the dead wolves' fur ruffled by the wind. "We did it."

Frost burbled happily then left Denali and flapped back over to Kumar.

Denali sheathed the hunting knife, put his mittens back on, and hurried over to his father.

Kumar remained unconscious, his head swollen, though the wolf bites on his arms and legs had healed over from Frost's licking.

Frost laid her head across Kumar's chest and whined.

The ground shook again. A deafening rumble filled the air. Above Denali and Frost, the side of the mountain collapsed in on itself and then blew outward in a giant explosion of superheated gases, ice, steam, and ash.

Chapter Ten

Kanvar gasped as the mountain in front of him blew into a huge column of billowing gray.

Dharanidhar veered away from the mountain, as the explosion of hot wind buffeted his wings. The trail they'd been following led right under the mushroom cloud to the slopes of the mountain. *I can't fly into that,* Dhar said. *You'll be burned.*

Kanvar found himself speechless in the magnitude of the destructive force. The hot air burned his lungs. His heart shriveled, and he hung his head in defeat.

A piercing cry like a terrified infant stabbed through his mind.

That's a hatchling. Dhar dove toward the ground at the base of the explosion, all hesitation gone. The baby's scream echoed in his mind, awaking memories of his own hatchling, barely out of its egg, crying out in fear before the human hunters murdered it.

The rising mushroom of ash and hot gases slowed, and then collapsed in on itself, flowing down the slopes in a burning whoosh. On the ground ahead, a single light shone out of the enveloping darkness.

Kanvar's long-coat started to smolder as Dhar sped toward the light, oblivious to the heat and power of the erupting volcano.

"Dhar!" Kanvar screamed as the heat and ash hit his face, and his hair started to melt.

Dhar reached up, pulled Kanvar from his riding harness, and sheltered him in his giant clawed hands. With Kanvar cocooned in his hands, Dharanidhar flew blind, the hatchling's screams guiding him.

Dharanidhar swooped below the boiling mass of ash and hot gas. Kanvar felt him land hard and slide across the ice. As he slid, he wrapped his body around the hatchling and lifted his wings to form a protective ball. The smell of sulfur made Kanvar gag as the wave of heat and ash washed over Dharanidhar, but Dhar's fire-resistant scales and hide blocked the main force of destruction. Kanvar was soaked instantly with sweat caused by the heat.

Dhar opened his claws and set Kanvar on the ground. For a moment it was dark inside the safe cocoon made by Dhar's body. Then a soft white light glowed to life. It came from the most beautiful Great White dragon hatchling Kanvar had ever imagined, shining from the dragonstone on her pearlescent forehead. Her shaking body was pressed up next to a young human boy. He had dark skin, glossy black hair, and big brown eyes that stared at Kanvar in shock. The front of his fur-line jacket was torn and spattered with blood. Kanvar recognized the boy's face from the image he'd seen in Eska's mind.

"Denali?" Kanvar held out a reassuring hand. "What happened? Are you hurt?"

Denali shook his head. "We fought a pack of snow wolves."

A clear picture of Denali's struggle against the wolves pressed into Kanvar's mind. Kanvar shuddered. "But you won. You defeated them."

Denali blinked back tears and looked down at a man lying on the ground in front of him. The man's arms and legs had been savagely torn, his leg broken and in a splint, and the back of his head swollen.

"Grandfather!" Kanvar dropped to his knees and leaned over Kumar Raza, listening for the sound of breathing, hoping to feel the soft touch of breath on his cheek. There it was, just the faintest tickle of air. Kumar was still alive. A spike of joy went through Kanvar. He'd arrived in time, just barely in time. But his grandfather was seriously hurt and would need a good healer to return him to health.

"Who are you?" Denali asked. "Are you all right? Your face is burned."

Kanvar didn't need to be told about the burns on his face made by the hot gas, he could feel the intensity of the stinging heat even now that Dhar had him shielded from the volcano. But Kanvar was a little stunned by the picture he got of himself from Denali's mind. His whole face was red and blistered and his skin swollen around his eyes. He was lucky the blast hadn't blinded him.

The hatchling burbled with concern and licked his face.

Kanvar flinched as the long white tongue slathered his cheeks and around his eyes. The touch of the freezing tongue stung his burns, but he let the hatchling lick him anyway. "Sure hope dragon saliva heals burns," he said.

Denali glanced up at the massive object that pressed around and over him. "But who are you? What is that?" His voice cracked.

Kanvar reached out and rested a reassuring hand on Denali's shoulder. "You've been through a lot, but you're going to be all right. My name is Kanvar. Technically, I'm your nephew. Kumar Raza is my grandfather."

"Raza?" Denali said the name as if he'd never heard it before. "My father's name is just Kumar."

"Raza is an honorific given him after he defeated a Great Red dragon. It mean's Great Dragon Hunter."

Kanvar eased his grandfather's torn clothing back to get a look at the wolf bites on his arms and legs. The hatchling had done a lot of licking. The wounds were bad, but had already started to heal, though they would leave terrible scars.

"And . . . what is *that* blocking us from the volcano?" Denali looked around at the wall of blue scales that surrounded them.

"*That* is a very large Great Blue dragon," Kanvar said. He didn't want to frighten Denali, but he couldn't really hide Dharanidhar from him. If Denali hadn't been so shocked by the wolves, the volcano, and his father's wounds, he probably would have responded in terror to the fact that a Great Blue dragon had curled around him.

A blue glow sprang to life from Dharanidhar's dragonstone and mixed with the gentle white from the hatchling's. Dhar had tucked his head down under his wings, and as the stone lit, it revealed his scarred and grizzled face and blank white eyes. Not to mention his sharp teeth and claws.

Denali let out a yelp, scooted back away from Dhar's giant head and foreclaws, and bumped up against his scaly tail. Denali froze for a moment, then pulled away from Dhar's body, shaking with fear.

The Great White hatchling let out a delighted purr, hopped over to Dhar, and rubbed her tiny face up against his massive one.

Dhar let out a contented rumble and stroked the baby dragon with a finger of his claw.

Denali took a deep breath and let it out slowly. "Frost likes him. She thinks he's come to help us. Does that mean he won't eat me?"

Kanvar looked up from his grandfather's pale face and icy skin to stare at Denali. "You-you can hear her talking? You're way too young to be bonded, and y-you can't be a Naga. Not unless your mother comes from Naga lines. I know my grandfather's ancestral line back twenty generations. You can't have gotten it from him."

Denali held his arms out to Frost. She ran back to him and wrapped her forearms and wings around him in a tight hug, resting her delicate head on his shoulder.

"Frost doesn't really talk to me with words," Denali said. "She just shares feelings. I don't know how to explain it. And I have no idea what a Naga is. All I know is that I couldn't have fought the snow wolves without her."

Kanvar wiped away the sweat that trickled into his eyes and sat back. He remembered all too well how he could feel the emotions of dragons even before he bonded to Dhar.

The ground rumbled and shook beneath him as the volcano spewed more ash into the air. He knew Dharanidhar could take the heat, but Kanvar still didn't feel safe. *We need to get out of here*, he told Dhar.

Dhar agreed. *Just as soon as you explain our relationship to Denali, so he understands that I'm a friend.*

Kanvar could feel the love that Frost and Denali shared with each other. It mirrored his own relationship to Dhar, though Kanvar would be lucky to get his arms around one of Dhar's fingers to give him a hug.

Dhar snorted in amusement.

Since Denali already seemed to understand about caring for a dragon instead of hating it, Kanvar hoped his explanation would go over well.

"Denali, a Naga is a human that bonds with a Great dragon. Once the bond is made, the human and dragon become one being. They feel what each other feel, share each other's thought and emotions. And if one of them is killed, the other will die also. I am a Naga, and this is Dharanidhar, the dragon I'm bound to." Kanvar reached behind him and rubbed the two fingers of his stubby hand against Dhar's jaw.

"Oh," Denali said.

Kanvar felt Denali's mind go blank for a moment as if he couldn't quite grasp what Kanvar had said.

Frost let go of Denali and scrambled back over to Dhar, flapping up to sit on his forehead and run sleek fingers over his glowing blue stone.

Denali's mind reconnected. "So, you think I'm a Naga because Frost and I understand each other?"

"Right," Kanvar said. "Normal humans can't read dragon thoughts or feel their emotions. But Dhar and I can do that, and we've come to help you. We need to get out of here, all right?"

Denali frowned. "But being a Naga sounds wonderful. Why was my father so alarmed when he thought Frost was talking to me? He said my life could be in danger. Is it dangerous bonding with a dragon?"

Kanvar's gut twisted. Now was not the best time to have this discussion, but he sensed Denali might not cooperate unless Kanvar explained. "No, it's not dangerous for a Naga to bond with a dragon. It's a beautiful transformation. The problem is that other humans don't see it as that. The bonded Nagas are powerful, and humans fear that power. They hate all Nagas and have sworn to kill them. My own mother—" Kanvar choked and couldn't speak again for a few moments.

"Your mother?" Denali prodded.

Kanvar swallowed and forced himself to talk. "When she found out I was a Naga, she gave me poison and told me to drink it. When I refused, she tried to shoot me with grandfather's crossbow. Lucky for me, it is too big for her and she missed. She did succeed at shooting my father in the back though. He almost died."

Kanvar licked his lips and wished he hadn't. The dragon saliva on his skin tasted like rancid fish. "Ugh." He rubbed his tongue off on his coat sleeve and succeeded in adding the taste of volcanic ash to the fish.

Frost chirped in amusement at him as he spit the ash out of his mouth.

Denali stared at Kanvar with big eyes. "My mother would never hurt me, and neither would my father."

Kanvar winced in remembering Devaj's insistence that Kumar would try to kill them all as soon as he got his memories back. Kanvar didn't want to argue with Denali, but he had to warn him about Kumar Raza.

"Your father is a very famous dragon hunter. He's killed quite a few Great Dragons. He is a senior member of the dragon hunter council. It's his job to hunt down and kill Nagas. That's why when Kumar found out that my father, my brother, and I were Nagas, my father erased his memories of us and sent him to live up here. Kumar would have tried to kill us. I'm sorry, Denali, but it's true."

"No. No it's not." Denali pulled a wicked-looking hunting knife from his belt. It was twice as long as the one Kanvar carried, though it was made from stone instead of steel. "I won't let you kill him. No matter what you say."

Kanvar scooted back, and Dhar closed a protective claw around him. Denali was smaller than Kanvar, and Kanvar knew he could beat Denali in a fight, knife or no knife, but Denali might get hurt.

"Denali, I didn't come here to kill Kumar Raza. I had a nightmare that his life was in danger, so I came to try and save him. Even though my father and brother told me not to, I came because Kumar is my grandfather, and I love him. I think it was wrong that my father erased his memories. I want to help him remember who he really is, even if that means he tries to kill me. I only told you how much he hates Nagas, because you need to know before I try to bring his memories back. He might turn against you. You should be prepared for that."

"He would never turn against me," Denali snapped. "Never. Besides, he didn't seem angry when he thought Frost was talking to me, just concerned for my safety." Denali lowered the stone knife and looked down at Kumar. "I think he's dying. He can't hurt anyone in this condition. We need to get him to Kapik, a wise man in our tribe. He knows a lot about healing wounds."

Kanvar squeezed out of Dhar's claw and went back to Kumar and ran his fingers over the lump on the back of his head. "I met Kapik. He was nice to me. We'll need to hurry and get Kumar to him though. His head isn't bleeding anymore, but the swelling concerns me. Besides, we have to get out of here right now, before the volcano buries us for good."

"How?" Denali gazed up at the dragon wings that covered them. "With the whole mountain coming down on us?" The ground rumbled and shook in response.

"Dhar, can you still fly?" Kanvar asked.

I can if we leave soon, before I get so much piled on top of me that I can't move. The problem is flying up without having you humans burned to a crisp. Not to mention our little girl here. The heat would kill her very quickly. Dhar rubbed a gentle finger down Frost's neck.

"Do you think we could all fit in your hands like you held me when we came down?"

Yes, but I won't be able to see. Still, I think you're right. It's our best chance of getting out of here. I'll fly straight up, and when I feel cool air, I'll open my hands a bit so you can climb out and see where we're going.

"Agreed," Kanvar said. "We're getting out of here, Denali. But we've all got to scoot together so Dhar can pick us up."

Denali nodded and he and Frost moved up close to Kumar. Kanvar eased to the ground beside them. Dharanidhar picked them up in one claw and cupped the other claw over the top. Then he stretched and tried to take flight. Kanvar felt a heavy weight on Dhar's shoulders and wings.

Groaning, Dhar forced his body up. Kanvar hoped it wasn't already too late.

Straining, Dhar pulled his massive back legs up under his torso and then pushed with all his might. The load that held him pinned, burst upward, and he leaped into the sky, flying straight up.

Kanvar could feel the hot ash and gas on Dhar's face. A plume of molten lava licked his wing and trickled down his back. Very hot, but not painful to the Great Blue dragon. It would have killed the humans if they hadn't been shielded in Dharanidhar's hands.

Dhar breathed hard as he beat his heavy wings, gaining altitude, up and up, and up some more. *How far up can all this ash go?* he growled.

The heat and the weight of ash and the lack of oxygen sapped his strength. His wing that had been broken a few months back started to ache.

Keep going, Kanvar said. He had to speak directly into Dharanidhar's mind because the thunderous sound of the volcano and Dhar's thick claws blocked out his voice. *Just a little higher.*

Dhar pushed himself higher. He didn't like flying blind. He feared that he'd get his directions messed up and run into something like he had when he crashed into the side of the mountain the first day he'd met Kanvar.

You're all right, Kanvar reassured him. *You can hear the roar of the eruption just behind you. Use the sound to guide your flight.*

Dharanidhar flapped harder and burst free from the volcano's cloud. Cold air flashed across his face and wings. He gasped. He was so high, there was not much oxygen to draw into his lungs. He opened his fingers a bit for Kanvar to see out. Kanvar saw the cold twilight sky all around him and the coast far off below.*Head for the coast,* he told Dharanidhar. *Stay upwind of the volcanic cloud.* Fortunately the wind was blowing eastward. *We should go straight back to Illulissat.*

Dharanidhar agreed. He twisted in the air and dove westward toward Illulissat on the coast.

Chapter Eleven

 Denali huddled against Frost. The glow of her stone helped fight back the fear and wonder he felt at being so tightly enclosed in the Great Blue dragon's claws, especially when the dragon opened his hands a crack and let Kanvar climb out onto his neck.

The cold wind sliced the air, and the dragon's body undulated up and down with each flap of his wings. The volcano still thundered behind them, spewing lava and ash into the air. The smell of sulfur mixed with the metallic scent of the Great Blue dragon.

Denali couldn't believe Kanvar willingly climbed out of the dragon's hand and onto his neck so far above the ground while going at such a fast speed.

Kanvar grinned at him and secured himself to the blue dragon's neck with a leather harness. Denali caught sight of the ground far below. The glacier had melted. A torrent of water carried chunks of ice and ash toward the sea. Lava seeped up from the fissure that had taken Iluq.

A pitiful howl sounded barely audible in the shadow of the thundering mountain. Denali caught sight of a fuzzy gray form, standing splay-legged on a bobbing piece of ice.

"It's Miki," Denali shouted. "He'll drown." The wind whipped his words away so neither Kanvar or the Great Blue dragon heard him. Frost's dragonstone blinked, and the blue dragon's stone blinked back in answer as if the two dragons were talking to each other. Dharanidhar folded his wings and dove toward the ground.

Frost let out a happy squeal as Dharanidhar snatched the frightened dog up in one of his back claws.

Denali heaved a sigh of relief and laid a hand on his father's chest. "Miki's alive."

Kumar remained as unconscious as he had been since the wolves had gotten a hold of him. Frost whined and licked at his wounds again, though they'd already healed over.

Denali leaned against the hard scales at his back. He had never imagined a dragon as big as Dharanidhar. And here he was flying, cupped in the dragon's hands. Part of him insisted he should be terrified. The other part could not get over the excitement of making friends with a second dragon and flying. Flying, like a sea bird. Heat and fire didn't seem to bother the blue dragon at all.

"We'd be dead right now if it weren't for Dharanidhar," Denali murmured to Frost. The blue dragon's name felt odd and unpronounceable on his tongue. "Will you tell him thank you, for me?"

Frost bobbed her head up and down, and her stone flashed. Denali rubbed her head and tried to push Kanvar's warning about his father out of his mind. But it wouldn't go. Kanvar really seemed to believe that Kumar would try to kill them. Denali didn't even want to think about it. It couldn't be true. But then, how could a mother try to shoot her own son? Could being a Naga be such a terrible thing? His concerns and fears tumbled around in his head until the dragon suddenly flared up and then settled to the ground.

Fearful shouts filled the air.

Dhar opened his claws and set Denali, Kumar, and Frost on the ground.

Denali found the men of his tribe, staring up at the dragon in shock, spears ready to throw.

Dharanidhar let out a warning growl.

Kanvar shouted something, but his Southerner accent made it impossible to tell what he said from so high up on Dharanidhar's neck.

The men drew their spears back while the rest of the tribe scrambled for the boats.

"No wait!" Denali cried, jumping up and stumbling toward the men. "The dragon is a friend. He saved my father and me."

Kapik lowered his spear and looked over at Kumar lying on the ground.

"Don't listen to him," Tartok shouted. "He's being controlled by that Naga up there." Tartok pointed to Kanvar. "Aim for the Naga. If you kill him, it will set the dragon free and it will fly away. It's our best chance."

"No," Denali cried.

The tribesmen ignored Denali and all except Kapik threw their spears at Kanvar.

Dharanidhar grabbed Frost in a protective claw and reared up on his hind legs. The stone spears clattered harmlessly against the scales on his chest. He let out a roar, then launched into the air and flew west.

Denali watched them go with a sinking heart. He felt most keenly the sudden separation from Frost and hoped she would be all right.

"You see what he's brought upon us," Tartok shouted and pointed at Kumar. "The animals vanish. The glacier melts. The mountain explodes in fire. And a Naga comes with a Great Blue dragon to make us all his slaves. Kumar is responsible. He must be a Naga as well. I say we kill him. Only his death will pacify the mountain."

Tartok snatched Kapik's spear from his hands and strode over to Kumar.

Denali pulled out his hunting knife and stood over his father. "I killed an entire pack of snow wolves, and I'll kill you too if you try to murder my father."

"You did not. Now, stand aside boy." Tartok pushed Denali out of his way and lifted the spear over Kumar's heart.

"No, don't let him," Denali pleaded with the other men of the tribe.

He saw only hate and fear in their eyes, even Atka who had been Kumar's best friend. Denali felt like he was facing another pack of snow wolves, only this time worse, these wolves were people he knew, his own tribe. Their betrayal lit a fire in him like the heat of the volcano. So this is what Kanvar had been trying to tell him. Everyone hated Nagas, even the Tuniits.

Yelling, Denali leaped on Tartok's back and pressed his hunting knife against Tartok's throat. Frost was no longer here to help. He'd have to save his father himself. "Drop the spear. My father is not a Naga."

Tartok dropped the spear, reached up, and tried to wrestle the hunting knife away from his throat.

Kapik picked up the spear and aimed it between Denali's eyes. "That Naga said Kumar was his grand-father. As much as I hate to admit it, Tartok is right. Let go of him, Denali. Don't make me have to kill you too."

"NO!" Eska's scream startled the men. They'd been so focused on Kumar, they hadn't notice her come up behind them. "Don't kill my son. Please don't."

Kapik lowered the spear. "Let Tartok go, Denali."

"Only if you promise not to let him kill my father." Denali's wrists hurt where Tartok had a hold of him, but he fought to keep the knife pressed to Tartok's throat.

Kapik turned to the other men of the tribe. "We are not killers. Never have any of us taken the life of a man before, let alone a boy. I say we release them. But they are no longer members of this tribe. If they come around, we drive them away. They no longer share our food or our camp or our protection. Let them be outcasts, but let them live."

The men muttered darkly, but nodded in agreement.

Denali eased the knife away from Tartok's throat. Tartok heaved him off his back, threw him to the ground, and kicked him in the side. "Naga brat. If I ever see you or your father again, I swear I *will* kill you."

He strode away, grabbing Eska's arm as he went. "You're mine now. Despite the fact you rejected me for that monster over there, I will forgive you and take you as my wife."

"No," Eska cried and tried to pull away from him. "I reject your offer. I don't want to be your wife."

Tartok grabbed her with both hands and shook her. "You have no choice. After belonging to that Naga. No one else will take you."

"I don't want anyone else," Eska shrieked. "I'm his wife, and his wife alone."

Tartok lifted a fist to beat her into submission, but Kapik grabbed his arm.

"You dare hit a woman?" Kapik said in disdain. "Tartok, take your hands off her. It's her choice. If she wishes to be outcast with Kumar, she may."

Tartok swore and stamped away toward the boats. Denali realized that the camp had already been taken down and the boats and sleds ready to go. The volcano rumbled in the distance. If the wind changed direction, the ash and fire would bury Illulissat. Even the Southerners were leaving, and quickly. They took the last supplies and people up into their big boat, let the sails out, and headed from the bay.

The Tuniits shoved off in their own boats and paddled away to the west, followed by the dogs and sleds on land. Denali choked back a cry of grief. He'd been so sure he'd be safe if only he could rejoin the tribe. Now he was alone again. Even Frost was gone.

Miki whined and lay down next to Kumar.

Eska rushed over to Denali and wrapped him in a tight hug. "I thought you were dead. Oh, I thought you were dead." She pushed his hood back and looked into his face as if to reassure herself that he was really there.

Denali pulled away. His heart cracked in his chest like melting sea ice. "What if I really am a Naga? Would you try to kill me too?"

His mother's eyebrows knit together. She looked at him closely and frowned. "Are you?"

Denali licked his lips. His hand tightened on the hunting knife. Alone, his mother could not kill him. But her rejection would feel worse than death. He had to know. He refused to hide what he was from his mother.

"I think I am. Kanvar does too."

Eska stepped back. Tears sprang into her eyes.

"But it's not Kumar's fault," Denali protested. "Kanvar said Kumar is a Naga hunter, and the Naga blood had to have come from you."

Eska shook her head and waved her mittened hands in denial. "There have never been any Nagas born into the Tuniit tribe. The stories of our past say that the father of our tribe came here with his family to escape the fighting at Stonefountain. Tuni was the poorest of the poor. A slave to the Nagas. He tricked one of them into giving him the elixir that would save his family from the coughing sickness. Then he ran away to the farthest place in the world from Stonefountain. A place the Nagas would never come. Great Gold dragons cannot live long in cold and darkness, and Nagas only bond with the Great Golds." Eska's frown deepened. "If Kumar's grandson is a Naga, he has enslaved the Great Blue dragon, taken control of its mind, and forced it to his will."

Denali's hand shook on the hunting knife. He'd never heard the tribe history before. That would have been part of the man ceremony when he turned twelve. "Kanvar said he is bound to the blue dragon, but that's not what's important. I need to know . . . will you still be my mother, will you still love me, if I am a Naga?"

Eska pressed her hands together. Tears made crystal ice patterns on her cheeks. "Denali I . . ." She looked over her shoulder as the last of the tribe disappeared from the bay. "It is forbidden for me to say this but—"

Her eyes brightened all of a sudden. "The punishment for telling a man this, is being outcast from the tribe. But we are already outcast, aren't we?"

Denali caught his breath. Maybe, just maybe his mother wouldn't hate him.

Eska grinned, showing her perfect white teeth. "In the woman ceremony the history is told a little differently. The women say that Tuni didn't trick the Naga to get the elixir. There was one Naga, one kind Naga, who cared about the poor people. This Naga gave up his own dose of the elixir willingly to save Tuni's daughter. And if that is true, then not all Nagas are evil. Kanvar told me he was going to save you and Kumar and bring you back to me. He did that. His face was so burned. He must have risked his life near the volcano to save you."

"Yes, he did." Denali swallowed a lump in his throat. A cold wind blasted him in the face, coming from the east, carrying the scent of scorched rock and sulfur.

"Then I consider him a friend, not an enemy."

"And me?" Denali said.

Eska swept Denali into a smothering hug. "You are my son, and I love you, Naga or not."

The whoosh of giant wings sounded overhead, and Dharanidhar settled to the ground next to Kumar. He lowered his neck so Kanvar could slide off.

"Denali, I'm sorry," Kanvar spoke before Denali could say anything. "I was just thinking about getting Kumar to Kapik as soon as possible. I should have known better than to let people see Dharanidhar. I'm so sorry. They made you outcast. It's my fault. How could I have been so stupid?"

Eska let go of Denali and hugged Kanvar.

"My grandson. My poor grandson. Look at you. Your face. Your arm. Your leg. And everyone hating you for being a Naga. How do you survive?"

Kanvar stood frozen in shock as if no one had ever hugged him before. His mouth opened, but no words came out. Frost flapped down from a perch on Dhar's shoulder and wrapped her forearms and wings around Eska and Kanvar's legs, joining in on the hug.

At the hatchling's cold touch, Eska squealed in shock and jerked away.

Frost let out a responding chirp of fear and buried her head against Denali. Denali patted Frost's back and spoke to his mother. "I bet Kanvar survives because he and Dharanidhar work together, just like Frost and I. I couldn't have survived that pack of snow wolves if Frost hadn't been with me."

Eska looked down at the little white dragon and then straight into Denali's eyes. "You *are* a Naga."

Denali shrugged. "I haven't bonded yet."

Kanvar smiled. "We'll deal with the whole bonding thing later. You're not old enough yet anyway. The wind has switched directions. We need to get out of here."

REBECCA SHELLEY

Chapter Twelve

Denali looked up to see a massive cloud of volcanic dust billowing toward them. Eska pointed to the loaded boat that waited in the water. "Help me get your father into the boat." She went to Kumar and lifted his shoulders. "Get his feet, Denali."

Denali wasn't sure that even with his mother's help he'd be able to carry Kumar to the boat. His father was a big man.

Kanvar seemed to read Denali's thoughts. He went to Eska and urged her to ease Kumar back to the ground. "Let Dhar do it. I think the boat is a good idea. It will make it much easier for him to carry everyone."

"Carry?" Eska's voice ended in a high squeak, and she stared up at the giant blue dragon.

Denali took her hand. "It's all right. He won't drop us. He can fly faster than the boat could go. I doubt we'd keep ahead of that cloud by paddling ourselves."

Dhar carefully picked up Kumar and laid him in the boat. Denali led his mother down to the water and held the boat while she got in, then he jumped in and hunkered down in the prow while his mother sat down on the bundle of their things in the stern. Miki leaped in too and settled himself alongside Kumar.

Frost flapped over and perched on the side of the boat. Her weight nearly flipped the small craft over, but Dhar lifted her away before the boat capsized. He put Frost back on his shoulder and lifted Kanvar up to his neck. Then he grabbed the boat up in one giant claw and took flight.

Ash fell to the ground where they'd been standing a moment before.

Denali gripped the sides of the boat with both hands and watched the cloud follow them, a roiling black and gray mass that filled the sky. Miki yipped with delight, stuck his head up over the edge of the boat, and let the wind blow in his face.

Dharanidhar did a good job of holding the boat steady while his wings beat up and down, but the rush of wind, the great height, and the movement, was too much for Eska. She stretched out in the bottom of the boat, wrapped her arms around Kumar, and buried her head against his chest.

Denali didn't know how he was going to explain that his father didn't even remember her, especially after she'd given up her position in the tribe to stay with him. He felt bad about that and yet happy she had stood by them, that she had not been like Kanvar's mother and tried to kill them. If she had even kept quiet, the Tuniit men would have done it for her. Denali might have taken Tartok down with him, but he wouldn't have survived an attack by the whole tribe.

I would not have let them hurt either of you, Kanvar's voice whispered into Denali's mind. Denali could barely make out the words, but knew Kanvar had spoken them. *The problem was trying to figure out a way to save you without hurting anyone else. But if it had come to a fight, we would have stood with you. I promise.*

Denali looked up to where Kanvar leaned against Dhar's neck. The wind whipped the edges of the silver long-coat out behind him. Denali recognized it as the one his mother had been making for his twelfth birthday. She'd meant to keep it a surprise, but Denali had seen her sewing on it a couple of times. He didn't mind that Kanvar wore it, though it was a bit small for him. At least it would keep him warm in the freezing wind.

Denali looked down and was surprised to see the coast end its westward sweep and cut sharply up to the northeast. Dhar left the coast behind and flew out over open water—a wide blue sea with chunks of ice floating among the waves.

Look behind you, Kanvar said into his mind.

Denali twisted so he was facing forward in the front of the boat and could gaze in the direction Dhar was flying them. A new coastline appeared. The waves crashed against towering black rocks and sent plumes of white water into the air. Inland, a thick carpet of pine trees covered the rocky ground.

"So many trees," Denali said in disbelief.

That's Kundiland, Kanvar said. *Hopefully the tribe will come this way. We saw thousands of seals and sea lions along this coast. Good thing too, because Dhar is starving.*

Denali laughed. "We all are. Aren't we Frost?"

He felt Frost agreeing with him. During the flight, she had remained on Dhar's shoulder, her own delicate wings spread into the wind, enjoying herself far too much. She let out a woeful whine when Dhar slowed and swooped into a sheltered sea grotto.

Kanvar had not lied. The place was packed with sea lions. Or at least it was packed for a moment. As soon as Dharanidhar flew in, the sea lions let out terrified barks and dove into the water. Six of the slower ones didn't make it. Dhar caught them up in his back claws and landed with them pinned beneath him.

He put the boat down on shore and set about dispatching the sea lions with alarming speed. He had four of them eaten before Denali could climb out of the boat. Dhar killed the last two sea lions and dropped them in front of Denali.

Frost flapped off his shoulder, landed on one of the dead sea lions and started her own feast. Miki jumped out of the boat and joined her.

"Thank you," Denali called up to Dhar. He got out his knife to gut and skin the sea lion. Dhar set Kanvar down and curled up to rest on a rocky shelf at the back of the grotto.

As soon as Denali had skinned the sea lion, Eska took over preparing it. Denali went to the boat to keep an eye on his father while she worked. Kanvar stayed behind and watched her pull their cooking things from the boat. She lit a basin of seal oil and put a pot of water overtop of it. Then she cut up chunks of sea lion and put them in to boil.

Denali's stomach rumbled as she prepared the food. Ignoring it, he slipped into the boat beside his father. "Father," he called softly, shaking Kumar. "Father?"

Kumar moaned. His eyes fluttered and then closed again. Denali got no further response no matter how he shook his father.

Eska left Kanvar to watch the boiling seal meat and came over to the boat. She examined all of Kumar's wounds, lingering longest over the swollen back of his head. "What happened?"

Denali explained about each of his father's wounds and how Frost had licked them and they'd healed over. "Even Kanvar's face looks a little better than it did a while ago, don't you think?"

Denali was glad to see the blisters had vanished from Kanvar's face and the swelling gone down around his eyes, though his cheeks were still red.

"Amazing," Eska said. "I guess Great White dragons do bring blessings." She let out a sharp breath and turned her attention back to Kumar. "So he hit his head on the ice when the dragon dropped him?"

"Yes. It was bleeding a lot until Frost licked the wound closed."

Eska grimaced and ran her hand over the lump which had continued to grow and now made Kumar's head too large and distorted. "I think it's still bleeding inside, putting pressure on his brain." She blinked back tears. "It will likely kill him in the end, since we have no way to stop it."

Kanvar dropped the spoon he'd been using to stir the boiling stew meat and hurried over to his grandfather. "No. There has to be a way to treat it. Kumar Raza can't die from a bump on the head." Denali's face had gone far too pale for Kanvar's liking.

Eska lifted Kumar's hand and pressed it against her cheek and made no attempt to argue with Kanvar. There was no need. Not even dragon saliva could stop bleeding beneath the skull.

Kanvar shook his head and balled his hand into a fist. "What do we do, Dhar?"

A lick of blue flame escaped Dharanidhar's mouth, blackening the back wall of the cave. Kanvar sensed he had an idea, but didn't want to share it.

"Dhar, what are you thinking?"

Dhar snaked his head up and looked down at Kanvar. A useless gesture. Whenever he looked at Kanvar like that, all he could see was himself through Kanvar's eyes. He did it anyway for the effect of seeming to look Kanvar in the face when speaking to him. *Parmver's elixer brought Devaj back to life after his heart had stopped beating. If anyone could heal your grandfather, it would be Parmver. But you know what that means.*

Kanvar stiffened and pressed his hand against his chest to still his thundering heart. "We would have to go to the palace."

Dhar nodded. *Last time we were there, they tried to make me a prisoner after we bonded. For all your father's fine talk, he is still bound to Rajahansa, and I'm certain Rajahansa does not approve of our bond. In the very least he'll try to lock me up for good. In the worst, he may try to break our bond and force you to bond to a gold dragon.*

"But that would kill us," Kanvar protested.

The thought of losing his link to Dharanidhar drove Kanvar to his knees.

It would most certainly kill me. You might survive as long as the bond was replaced quickly enough. Parmver does have his elixer after all. Dharanidhar's bitter thought made Kanvar shudder. Dhar wrapped his claw around Kanvar and lifted him into the air away from Denali, Kumar, and Eska. Smoke seeped from between his jaws. *I will take Kumar to the palace if you want me to. I know how much your grandfather means to you.*

Kanvar wrapped his arm around the top of Dhar's claw and looked up into his friend's scarred face. "You would risk imprisonment and death for a dragon hunter like Kumar Raza?"

Dharanidhar snorted. *It might be worth it to see Amar have to face his nemesis. The king of the Nagas against the king of the dragon hunters, who do you suppose will win? In the very least it will be entertaining.*

Dhar's amusement at pitting the two men against each other did not make Kanvar feel any better. "You're right. It's a stupid idea. We can't take Kumar there."

Kanvar looked down at Kumar. Eska and Denali sat beside him. Tears streaked both their faces. Even the baby dragon and the dog whined in sorrow.

Then you must bid your grandfather goodbye. I do not think he will ever wake again. Dhar lowered Kanvar back toward the ground.

"No, wait." A desperate kind of crazy washed over Kanvar. "I-I can't give up on my grandfather. We can't let him die. Please. Whatever the risk, we should take it."

Dharanidhar lifted his head and breathed a long spurt of blue fire up at the ceiling. Then he laughed a deep booming laugh that echoed through the grotto. *That's just the kind of thinking that drove you to bond with me. It's what I like most about you, Kanvar. You're always willing to throw your own life straight off a cliff to save someone else. Too bad for me, my life is bound to yours now. But I'm content with that. Let me rest, and then we'll fly hard for the golden palace.*

Dhar put Kanvar on the ground then tucked his head under his wing and forced himself to sleep.

Kanvar limped over to the grieving family. "Dhar has agreed to take Kumar to Parmver."

Denali looked up at Kanvar with his big brown eyes. "Who is Parmver?"

"The Naga that gave Tuni the elixer that saved his daughter's life." Last time Kanvar had been at the palace, he had seen the event through Parmver's own memories.

"A thousand years ago?" Eska said in disbelief.

"He's very old. You should see his dragon. I don't know how he can even move, let alone fly. But Parmver is a good man, and I trust him." No need to mention Kanvar's distrust of his own father or what might happen if Parmver was able to heal Kumar. "As soon as Dhar has rested we'll go. We may have to stop at least one more time before we get there. It took us three days to reach Illulissat. But Dhar intends to try and fly faster this time with fewer breaks." Kanvar rested a grateful glance on Dharanidhar's curled body. He could not have asked for a truer friend in all the world.

"Then we should eat now while we can," Eska said. "Come on, both of you boys."

Eska served them the boiled sea lion, but Kanvar hardly tasted it as he ate. He hadn't intended to take Kumar to the palace, just return his memories.

After Kumar remembered who he was, Kanvar had planned to take him back to Varna to be with Mani, Kanvar's mother.

From Varna Kumar would not have much chance of finding the golden palace. It was hidden deep in the Kundiland jungle where humans had never reached. Only the Nagas and gold dragons knew its location.

Rajahansa, the Great Gold Dragon King, would be furious when Kanvar showed up with Kumar.

Chapter Thirteen

Kanvar strained to see through the night's darkness as Dharanidhar glided just above the jungle canopy. Insects and frogs made the air throb with their buzzing and croaking. Grateful for the warmer climate, Kanvar had shed the long-coat, giving it back to Eska. The sweet scent of greenery and flowers rose from the trees. Kanvar was glad to return to the jungle. It felt so very alive compared to the frozen north.

Trying to be helpful, Frost set her stone alight. Dhar reached up and grabbed her off his shoulder, covering the light with his massive hands.

Frost, Kanvar chided. *We want it to be dark. That's why we waited until after nightfall. We don't need every Great Gold dragon in the entire valley after us.*

While Dhar had flown them down the Kundiland coast, Kanvar and Dhar had decided it would be best to arrive at the palace unnoticed. Kanvar kept their minds hidden from the Great Gold dragons with a strong shield as Dharanidhar neared the cliff face that held the golden palace. They knew from their last time here that Parmver had a private lab in a natural cave near the base of the cliff. Dhar had reached it in secret before and planned to do so again. Kanvar hoped Frost's bright light had not woken any of the sleeping gold dragons.

Dhar carried the boat with Eska, Kumar, Denali, and Miki in his other foreclaw.

As they drew closer to the cliff face, Kanvar caught sight of a dark crack in the rocks. *There it is, Dhar.*

Dharanidhar corrected his course to fly into the crack. It looked small from a distance, but up close Kanvar could see it was big enough for Dhar to fly into and settle to the ground in the center of the cavern.

Kanvar strained to hear any sound or sense the thoughts of any approaching gold dragons. *I don't think they noticed us*, he said as Dhar helped him down.

Dhar rumbled in agreement.

Kanvar limped over to the boat as soon as Dhar set it on the ground. "Denali," he whispered. "Stay here and look after Eska and Frost." He'd already explained to Denali how angry the Great Gold dragons might be about Kanvar bringing Kumar to their stronghold.

"But I want to come with you," Denali said. "I want to stay with my father, and I'd like to meet Parmver."

"I'm sure Parmver would be very excited to meet you too. But not right now. We need him to heal Kumar. Then we can take Kumar to safety. There's a village we'll go to after Parmver gives him the elixer. The villagers have a way to call the gold dragons to come and get you. Then you can meet Parmver. All right?"

Denali shook his head. "You're not taking my father anywhere without me."

"Don't be unreasonable. You need to stay here and keep your mother safe," Kanvar hissed. Not that he wouldn't mind having Denali by his side. That would be great, but it would get far too complicated with Frost, Eska, and Miki along as well.

"I'll be all right," Eska whispered.

Kanvar had gradually grown to understand her and Denali's accent without having to read their minds.

"I know we can't all go up there. I can stay here alone with Miki and Frost. Your blue dragon can protect us. But let Denali go."

"All right." Kanvar relented. "Everyone out of the boat." *No Frost. You have to stay here.*

Denali stood and stepped from the boat, giving his mother a hand out. Miki whined and remained lying beside Kumar. Dhar plucked Miki out of the way and then scooped Kumar from the boat.

"This way." Kanvar led Denali to the edge of the chamber where a large double door marked the entrance to Parmver's lab.

Set back in the rock a few yards away, a narrow staircase led up to the palace far above.

Kanvar eased the lab doors open, expecting pitch blackness inside. He was surprised to see what looked like a small glass globe hanging from the ceiling. White light emanated from the globe almost like the light from Frost's dragonstone.

"What kind of magic is that?" Denali stepped into the lab.

"I have no idea." Kanvar followed him in. The light illuminated a room lined with shelves. One whole shelf was covered with books and scrolls. Another with jars full of dead insects, animal parts, and crushed plants. Drying plants hung from the edges of the ceiling. A steel counter stretched the length of one wall and held all kinds of flasks and vials and curious metal objects like the collapsible stove Kanvar had seen his father use to heat water. In the center of the room, beneath the glowing light, sat an empty steel table. A dusting of yellow pollen covered the surface as if Parmver had been crushing dried flowers on it.

Kanvar wiped the pollen away and called to Dharanidhar with his mind. *There's a place you can lay him in here. Set him down and then I'll try to call Parmver without my father hearing.*

Dhar's fist barely fit through the wide double doors, but he got it in and laid Kumar on the table. *Good luck,* he told Kanvar. Then withdrew to the cavern and wrapped himself around Eska and Miki. Frost flew up to land on his head, but he pulled her down again before she could light the whole chamber.

Denali stood to one side of the table, gripping Kumar's arm. Kumar had not woken during their swift flight down to the jungle.

"Well?" Denali prodded Kanvar.

"Right. I sure hope this works." Kanvar closed his eyes so he could focus, then he let down the shields that protected his mind and sent his thoughts out in search of Parmver. He felt the gold dragons first and shied away from them, looking for human minds. He found his father, sleeping, and veered away before making contact. He sensed two other Nagas, whom he'd never met. They were also asleep. So was Aadi, the village boy that Parmver hoped would be a Naga.

Kanvar's mind moved on, washing into Devaj's who was awake, reading a book by lamplight. Devaj dropped the book and jumped to his feet. *Kanvar?*

Kanvar threw up a shield between them and hoped Devaj had not sensed exactly where Kanvar was. Kanvar shuddered. He liked Devaj, trusted him, but Devaj was too close to their father. If he found out Kanvar was this near the palace he would wake Amar for sure.

"Kanvar, are you all right?" Denali whispered.

Kanvar took a deep breath and wiped the sweat from his forehead. His heart thumped too loudly in his chest, and his head started to ache from too much use of his powers. "I-I'm all right. Just give me a moment more."

Refocusing his mind, he went back to searching for Parmver. He found him dreaming he walked the golden halls at Stonefountain, holding hands with a pretty young Naga girl. The two kissed beneath an arch entwined with silver roses. Kanvar hesitated for a moment, unwilling to shatter such a perfect dream. As soon as the young couple's lips parted, Kanvar spoke into Parmver's mind. *Parmver, I need your help.*

The girl vanished. Parmver groaned. *Who? What?*

It's me, Kanvar. I need your help. But don't tell anyone I'm here.

Here where?

In your lab.

Parmver crawled out of bed and stretched his aching body. Connected to Parmver's mind, Kanvar got a vivid feel for how old Parmver really was. Old and feeble, but unwilling to let go of life and move on.

Parmver lifted a velvet wall between his aches and pains and Kanvar's mind. *You're here. Good. I was afraid you might never come back. There is so much I need to teach you.*

I'm not here to learn, Kanvar protested. *My grandfather's dying. He needs your elixer to heal him. But you can't tell my father. He'd be furious that I brought Kumar Raza here.*

Parmver recoiled. *You brought the Great Dragon Hunter here?*

He's dying, Parmver. Please. He's no threat in this condition. Just give him some of the elixer, and I'll take him away. Kanvar's head began to hurt even more. He'd never used his powers like this before.

Kanvar. Parmver used his own mind to sooth Kanvar's aching head. *There is no one elixer that heals everything. Medicine doesn't work like that. Specific tinctures do specific things, and most things cannot be healed in an instant.*

But you have to try. Kanvar opened his eyes and looked down at his grandfather, so Parmver could see the swelling on the back of Kumar's head.

Parmver swore. *Stay there.*

The connection to Kanvar's mind broke off.

As soon as Kanvar lost the connection to Parmver's mind, a splitting pain knifed through his head.

He gasped.

"Is he coming? Will he help us?" Denali asked.

Kanvar staggered against the bookshelf and pressed his hand to his forehead. "I-I-I-I don't know. He said to stay here. He might be waking up all the Nagas."

Denali pulled out his hunting knife. "Then we'll deal with them. I won't let them hurt my father."

"You don't understand. They can control your mind, your thoughts, your body, even your emotions, and I don't know how to use my powers enough yet to block them. That knife will be useless against them." The pain in Kanvar's head was a sharp reminder that he had never been trained how to use his powers correctly beyond the most basic idea of how to build a mind shield.

The thump of running steps sounded on the rock steps outside the lab. "That can't be Parmver," Kanvar said. "He's too old to run like that."

Despite what he'd told Denali, Kanvar pulled his crossbow from its harness on his back and fought to get it loaded as the footsteps neared the bottom of the stairs. Maybe he could keep control of his own mind long enough to get off at least one shot.

Kanvar lifted the crossbow just as Devaj barreled into the room. Devaj jerked to a stop and spread his hands as soon as he saw Kanvar's crossbow pointed at his heart. "Whoa there, little brother. You don't need that. I'm not going to hurt you."

Kanvar eased his finger away from the trigger, but kept the crossbow pointed at Devaj. "Don't call father. If you've already wakened him, tell him never mind. It's nothing. He can go back to sleep."

"Kanvar, relax. You know father won't hurt you. He—" Devaj caught sight of Kumar lying on the table. His mouth worked, but no more words came out.

"Tell father to go back to sleep," Kanvar ordered.

Devaj shook his head. "I didn't wake him. I came down here by myself. Just me. All right?"

"I need Parmver."

Kanvar's hand shook on the crossbow.

Devaj reached out and pushed the tip down toward the floor. "I sense that he's coming. But he's an old man. Give him a minute." Devaj walked around Kanvar to get to the table.

Denali stepped in his path, knife raised.

Devaj cocked his head to the side and looked Denali over. "And who are you?" he said in a soft voice.

"Get back," Denali said, jabbing the knife in Devaj's direction. Not close enough to cut. Just a warning. "I won't let you kill him."

"Kanvar, tell your friend here that I'm not going to kill anyone. I just want to see what's wrong." Devaj did not try to push the knife aside as he'd done Kanvar's crossbow.

Kanvar took a deep breath to steady his nerves. He hadn't meant to involve Devaj in this. But if Devaj had not wakened Amar, there might be some hope left that Kanvar could get Kumar healed and away in secret.

"Denali, this is my brother, Devaj. He's on our side, I hope." Kanvar removed the crossbow bolt from the groove and rested the tip of the bow on the ground. "Devaj, Grandfather is hurt bad. We need Parmver to help him."

"I can see that," Devaj said, his voice soothing. His mind sent a wash of emotion over Kanvar and Denali, making them feel that they could trust him. "Welcome to the palace, Denali. You can put that knife away. You won't need it here."

Denali blinked and slid the knife back in its sheath at his waist.

"D-don't use your powers on us," Kanvar said. He tried to shield his mind from his brother, but Devaj had already gotten inside.

"It's all right, Kanvar." Devaj searched Kanvar's mind for exactly who and what Denali was. Devaj started in surprise. "He's a Naga? Kumar's son is a Naga? How in the world?" Devaj's mind slipped away from Kanvar's.

Kanvar gasped and rebuilt his shields.

"Sorry about that, little brother. I know you don't like anyone else's mind in your own, but I had to make sure Denali didn't gut me with that very-sharp-looking knife." Devaj stepped around Denali and circled the table, staring in wonder at Kumar.

"Free Denali's mind too," Kanvar said.

Devaj pursed his lips and shook his head. "I don't think so. Not yet. I'm not hurting him. I just let him know I'm a friend, and he can trust me."

"Can he really?" Kanvar didn't like the way Devaj was looking at Kumar as if he'd never seen his own grandfather before.

"Grandfather?" Devaj brushed his fingers across Kumar's brow and then felt the swollen place on the back of his head. "Grandfather, you have Naga blood? But how?"

"I was wondering when you'd figure it out." Parmver's raspy voice made Kanvar jump. The old man hobbled into the room with the use of a cane. He seemed weaker than the last time Kanvar had seen him.

Devaj turned and stared at Parmver. "You knew?"

Parmver rolled his eyes and went over to Kumar. "Really Devaj, have you forgotten all your lessons?"

Devaj stepped aside and let Parmver get a look at Kumar's head. "I don't understand."

"Neither do I," Kanvar said.

"I don't understand any of this," Denali chimed in. "I just barely found out that I'm a Naga and am still not clear on what that means exactly."

Parmver patted Denali's arm with a wrinkled hand. "Don't worry. You have time. I'll teach you everything you need to know." He turned his attention to Devaj. "I'm going to need your help with Kumar. Take the children out, then come back and lock the doors."

"Not a chance. I'm not leaving," Kanvar said.

"I'm not a child," Denali said. "I'll be twelve soon."

Parmver snorted. "Take them out quickly," he told Devaj. "We don't have much time. It might already be too late."

Devaj put an arm on Denali's shoulder and guided him out the door. Denali's eyes glazed over, and he went without argument.

Kanvar moved to the back of the lab, slid the bolt back into the slot, and lifted the crossbow to point at Devaj. "Don't even try that with me. I might have a splitting headache, but I'm not letting you back into my mind again. I'm staying here. However Parmver plans to heal Grandfather, I'm going to help too."

"Kanvar, don't be stupid," Devaj said. "You'll just get in the way. If Grandfather has any chance at all of surviving, you need to trust Parmver to treat him."

"I'm not leaving," Kanvar said.

Ignoring the argument, Parmver started pulling instruments from the work table. Shocking things like a hand-drill, leather straps, and a very sharp knife.

"Wh-what are you going to do?" Kanvar asked.

Parmver left off readying his things and hobbled over to Kanvar. He pushed aside the crossbow and looked Kanvar in the eyes. "There is bleeding inside his skull. The pressure is destroying his brain. Every moment we wait, he has less chance of recovery. I have to cut a hole in his skull and put in a shunt, a hollow tube, to drain the fluids. It is not going to be pretty. I suggest you go out with Denali." Parmver gave Kanvar's right arm a squeeze and then went back to work.

"Devaj, secure him to the table. If he wakes, give him this tincture to kill the pain. Do whatever you must to keep his head perfectly still." Parmver set a vial of green liquid on the table beside the instruments.

Devaj nodded in understanding and used the leather straps to tie Kumar to the table.

Kanvar's gut twisted, and he limped over to the doors. Parmver was right; he couldn't watch this. "P-Promise me you're trying to help him."

"Kanvar," Parmver said. "I swear by Stonefountain we're trying to save your grandfather not hurt him. But this is the only way."

Kanvar eased out of the lab and slumped to the ground against the rock wall. Devaj closed the doors and barred them from the inside.

Denali still stood where Devaj had left him. After a moment, he blinked and whirled toward the doors, fumbling to pull his knife back out. He saw the doors closed and Kanvar sitting next to them. "What . . . what happened? How did I get out here?"

Kanvar shrugged. "I told you, they can control your mind. The only thing that can stop a really powerful Naga is a singing stone. And believe me, you and I wouldn't want to use one even if we had one. It would hurt our minds as much as Devaj and Parmver's."

"What are they doing in there?"

"Trying to save him." Kanvar pressed his face to his knees and wished the headache would go away.

"Are you sure?" Denali came over and sat down beside him.

"I think so. I hope so. But even if they try, it doesn't sound like Kumar has much chance."

"Any chance is better than none." Denali folded his arms across his chest and stared at the doors. A muffled shout of pain came from within.

Chapter Fourteen

Denali watched as a pale golden glow filtered into the cavern. There had been silence in the lab for a long time since Kumar's first shout. Denali strained to hear what was taking place behind the doors, but whatever Parmver and Devaj were doing, they were doing it in quietly.

Leaving the pouch with the Great White dragonstone slung over his shoulder, Denali eased his jacket off and wished he had something to wear other than seal furs. He'd never dreamed anywhere could be as hot as this place. Denali couldn't see Frost from where he stood, just the Great Blue dragon curled around her, but Denali could tell the heat was making Frost sick and dizzy. She would not be able to stay here much longer. And still there was silence from the lab.

"It's getting light," Denali said.

Kanvar raised his head from his knees. "It does that here. The sun rises and sets like its supposed to, unlike in the Great North."

"It feels strange, like summer has come early." Denali paced in front of the doors. He had to do something. Parmver was taking too long to heal his father.

"It always feels like summer here, Denali." Kanvar looked as worried as Denali felt.

"Well, I'm dying from the heat, and so is Frost." Denali strode back down into the center of the cavern to the baby dragon curled up asleep in one of Dharanidhar's claws. Eska woke as Denali approached.

"Is he alive? Did Parmver heal him?" She got up and pulled her cook pot from the boat. "Are you hungry?"

"Yes, I'm hungry," Denali lied. His stomach was too twisted with worry to eat anything, but he knew his mother loved cooking. It would give her something to do while they waited.

Miki whined, indicating he was hungry too.

Eska lowered the pot she'd just picked up. "You didn't answer."

Denali pointed across the cavern to the upper edge where Kanvar still sat beside the doors. "He's in there with Parmver. It's been hours. We haven't heard anything. Parmver wouldn't let Kanvar and I stay with Father while he treated him. I don't know if Father is still alive or not."

Eska wrapped an arm around Denali's shoulders. Sweat ran down her face. "If they're still in there, it means he still has a chance. If he had died, Parmver would have come out and told us."

Denali forced himself to smile. He wanted to believe his mother.

The sound of great wings flapping outside the cave made Denali look up. He squinted into the sunlight but couldn't see anything.

Dhar rumbled, stood upright, and spread his wings.

A gold dragon slid into the cave's shadow. It dove past Dharanidhar and landed in front of the lab doors. Denali gasped. The dragon was so beautiful. Shimmering gold. Larger than the Great White he-dragon had been, but still much smaller than Dharanidhar.

Devaj opened the lab doors.

The gold dragon reached in, lifted Kumar off the table, cradled him carefully against his golden chest, and darted back out of the cave.

"No!" Kanvar yelled, jumping to his feet. "Devaj, what are you doing?"

"It's all right," Devaj said loud enough for everyone to hear. "Kanvar, stay calm. Dharanidhar—" Devaj lifted a placating hand toward the blue dragon who had sucked in an angry breath. Blue fire crackled between his teeth. "—don't kill anyone. That was just Elkatran, my dragon. He's moving Kumar to more comfortable quarters in the palace."

"But father will kill him," Kanvar protested.

Parmver shuffled out of the lab. He looked tired, and his shoulders stooped even more than they had before.

"Of course he won't, Kanvar. Don't be silly. Kumar is your father's best friend. It broke his heart when he had to send Kumar away to keep you boys safe."

"But . . . but . . ." Kanvar spluttered.

Eska left her pot and strode across the chamber to Parmver. "Are you Parmver?"

"I am." Parmver nodded and held a gnarled hand out to Eska. "And who are you, my dear?"

"I'm Kumar's wife, Eska. Kanvar said you gave Tuni the elixer that saved his daughter's life from the coughing sickness at Stonefountain. Is that true?"

"Well," Parmver cleared his throat, "I didn't really know the man's name. But I did give someone my dose of medicine for the cough."

"Then I trust you," Eska said. "Kanvar, what are you doing with that weapon?"

Denali realized Kanvar had pulled out his crossbow and was bent over, loading it. "I-I can't let my father hurt us. He will chain us, enslave us. Kill us." Kanvar was shaking so much, he could barely get the crossbow bolt into the groove.

Denali could see no reason for Kanvar's actions. Devaj felt like a friend, and Parmver was a harmless old man and might have saved Kumar's life. Frost hopped over to Denali and rubbed her head against his chest.

Parmver reached out and turned Kanvar toward him. He stared into Kanvar's eyes for a moment before speaking. "Kanvar, those are Akshara's memories. Not your own. Where did you get them?"

Dharanidhar let out a blast of blue fire that blackened the cave wall above Parmver's head. His dragonstone flashed a deep blue, and Denali sensed that all Great Blue dragons carried Akshara's memories. Denali felt the weight of great chains upon his wrists and ankles and the pain of a Naga's mind raking through his own, forcing him into submission.

"Stop!" Parmver shouted.

A fuzzy warmth from Parmver blocked Denali from feeling any more painful memories. "You're hurting the children, Dharanidhar. Can't you tell? You've got to learn how to control your mind, to control your powers."

Dharanidhar settled to the ground on all fours and shook his massive head. Miki whimpered and went to hide in the farthest corner of the cave.

"None of that happened to you, Dharanidhar." Parmver hobbled down closer to the Great Blue dragon.

"Those aren't your own experiences. No Naga has ever chained you or hurt you. Everything you're feeling happened long ago to some other dragon. The Great Gold King never should have treated his subjects that way, and he paid the price when Akshara got his claws on him. But it's all over. Finished a thousand years ago. You don't need to keep passing these memories down to the next generation."

Dharanidhar let out a defiant roar as if to say that the Great Blues would never let the pains of Stonefountain be forgotten lest they should be repeated.

Denali pressed his hands to his head.

Devaj's strong arm wrapped around him and led him away from the angry blue dragon and up the stone staircase with Eska at their heels.

"It's all right," Devaj whispered. "Let Parmver handle this." He pressed a hand against Denali's head, blocking all feeling of the dragons below.

"But." Denali tried to turn back. Kanvar was still down there.

Devaj kept him moving up the stairs. "It's an old feud and doesn't concern you. Kanvar will be all right. Your father needs you more right now."

"But he doesn't even remember my mother and me," Denali blurted out. "Ever since he hit his head, he forgot us. He remembered you though. He thought I was you."

"Well, it was a pretty hard crack to the head," Devaj said. "But that's why he needs you now. You can remember for him."

Devaj opened a door and led Denali out into a vast golden hall.

Eska gasped and ran her hand up one of the columns. "It's gold. Real gold."

Denali turned so he could take it all in. Sunlight poured in through giant arched windows. Windows big enough that even Dharanidhar could fly in through them and land on the gold-covered floor. A high ceiling was held up by columns spaced far enough apart that the dragons could fly or walk between them at will. He could see the great hall stretching on in a semicircle around the cliff face. More chambers and rooms had been carved out of the cliff itself, ones with giant doors and others with human-sized doors.

Frost scrambled up from the stairs and threw herself at Denali, chiding him for abandoning her.

"Sorry, Frost." Denali rubbed her dragonstone in apology and followed Devaj further into the palace. He couldn't believe the brightness and the majesty of the place. Despite the heat, he felt a sense of rightness wash over him, like he'd come home to a permanent camp that would not move with the seasons like the Tuniits had. He spread his arms and let the sun soak into his bare chest. He'd come home and had no desire to ever leave.

Frost whimpered and wrapped her forearms around him. She did not like this place. It was too hot and made her sick and dizzy.

"It's all right, little one," Devaj said. "You won't have to stay here. You would grow sick and die from the heat. In just a moment I'll have Elkatran take you back north to your parents."

"Her parents are dead." Denali patted Frost's back. "She can't go back. There is a volcano covering all the land with ash. The animals have fled to Kundiland. If she went there she would starve to death like her parents."

A man wrapped in a golden glow with a crown on his forehead and a shimmering robe like tiny gold dragon scales, came around a pillar and strode up to them. "What's this?" he asked Devaj.

"Good morning, Father." Devaj flashed the man a wide grin. "This is Eska, Kumar's wife, and his son, Denali. Kanvar found them and brought them back with him. Denali, Eska, this is Amar, the Great Gold King."

Amar's brow wrinkled. "He brought them here? And Kumar too?" He looked around as if expecting an attack.

The smile faded from Devaj's face. "Kumar's hurt. Parmver treated him, but I don't think—" Devaj glanced sideways at Eska and didn't finish his sentence.

Amar's frown deepened. "Where's Kanvar. Why can't I feel him?"

"He's down in the cavern with his . . . dragon and Parmver. There seems to be a bit of a problem. Parmver's sorting it out."

"A problem?" Amar glanced toward the staircase.

More than a bit of a problem, Denali wanted to shout, but he kept his mouth closed. His mind spun, remembering one of the few lucid things his father had said after the battle with the Great White dragon. Kumar had said that if he died, Denali was to find Amar. That Denali might need him. And this man, this king, standing in front of Denali was Amar. Kanvar's father. But Kanvar had said nothing about his father being a king.

Devaj gave a nervous shrug. "It seems that Akshara passed certain vivid memories on to all of his pride, and Kanvar has those memories now as well. As if . . . he had experienced Akshara's life himself."

Red crept around the edges of Amar's face. "Well, that would explain Kanvar's distrust of me." He clenched his fists.

Frost whimpered.

Amar's eyes settled on the little hatchling. He dropped to his knees and ran a hand down her slender neck. "And aren't you a beautiful one. So far from home. Aadi!" he called over his shoulder.

A boy about Denali's age raced out of one of the smaller chambers and skidded to a stop next to Amar. "Yes, Majesty?"

"Take this precious girl to the ice chamber and ask Bellori to bring her some food." Amar continued to stroke Frost reassuringly.

"You can't put a baby dragon in there," Aadi protested. "With all that ice you have brought down from the north. She'll freeze."

"That's the point. White dragons need the cold." Amar got to his feet and nudged Frost away from Denali. "Go with Aadi, Frost. I'll take care of Denali for you."

Frost's dragonstone pulsed.

"Yes, and Kumar. I promise," Amar said. "But you need to cool off quickly, before you get sicker."

Frost let out a warble of agreement, hopped over, and took Aadi's hand. Denali felt horrible watching her walk away with Aadi. But if there was somewhere she could cool down, that would be better.

"She'll be all right, Denali." Amar put a hand on his shoulder, and he felt a wave of peace wash over him.

Devaj cleared his throat. "Kumar is going to need you, Father. We've put him in the chambers you prepared for Kanvar."

Amar nodded. "Take Eska and Denali to him. I'll come in a minute." He strode off toward the staircase.

Chapter Fifteen

Kanvar got his crossbow loaded but didn't know what good it would do him. He couldn't shoot Parmver, and if his father came down those steps, Amar would be able to take it from him as easily as Devaj had pushed it aside.

Out in the cavern, Parmver was talking to Dharanidhar. The words seemed meaningless as Kanvar's mind drifted from the present into Akshara's memories and back. Akshara had been the Great Blue dragon who had clawed the singing stones free from the walls at Stonefountain to give to his followers for the uprising. Akshara was a hero, and Kanvar felt blessed to have his memories from Dharanidhar's mind. But . . . Kanvar shook his head and tried to focus on what was important now. Devaj had moved Kumar. Taken him somewhere in the palace. Kanvar hadn't been able to see if Kumar was alive or dead, if the surgery had worked or not.

And if Kumar was still alive, would Amar leave him that way?

"Grandfather." Kanvar kept his crossbow out and limped to the stairs. His deformed left leg always made climbing stairs difficult, and these were narrow and uneven. He needed his right hand against the wall to steady himself. But he couldn't do that and carry the crossbow. Not unless he disarmed it and put it back in its harness.

Behind him in the cavern, Dhar stopped roaring. His voice dropped to a worried grumble.

Kanvar's foot slipped, and he fell backward. Parmver caught him and eased the crossbow from his fingers.

"How about I carry this for you?" Parmver said. "Hold onto the wall there and take it easy. Nice and slow. You're grandfather is stable for the moment. There is still much to do to help him, but he won't die before you reach the top of the stairs."

Kanvar steadied himself against the pitted stone of the wall. "Are you sure?"

"Yes, I'm sure." Even with as old as Parmver was, he handled the long staircase better than Kanvar.

"Tell my father not to hurt him."

"Your father won't hurt him. I promise."

"Tell him to leave Kumar's mind alone. Not to make him forget again."

Parmver cleared his throat but didn't answer.

Kanvar twisted back to look at him and almost fell again. Parmver couldn't steady him this time since he had one hand on his cane and the other on Kanvar's crossbow. He pressed a shoulder against Kanvar's chest until Kanvar got his balance. "Should have had Dharanidhar fly you up there," he muttered.

That made Kanvar angry. "I can do anything anyone else can do." He dragged his twisted leg up the next step and the next. He was gasping for breath by the time he reached the top and stepped out into the palace. He blinked in the bright light. He'd forgotten how blinding the palace was.

As soon as his eyes adjusted, he saw his father waiting for him next to the closest pillar. He wore an even grander robe than the one he'd had on when he met Kanvar at the empty Maran Colony. He stood very still, his hands at his sides, his eyes fixed on Kanvar, and his mind locked tightly away.

"Where is Kumar?" Kanvar demanded.

"He's in your quarters." Amar spoke so softly Kanvar could barely hear it.

"I have quarters here?"

"Of course you do. This is your home."

"No." Kanvar shook his head. "I live with the Great Blue dragons. Not here."

Parmver chuckled, removed the bolt from Kanvar's crossbow and pressed the weapon into Kanvar's hand.

"It's cold up in the mountains," Amar said. "Winter's coming. Frost will be happy about that, I'm sure. But you . . . you'll need somewhere warm." He still hadn't moved more than just to blink now and then. Kanvar recognized it has a hunting technique. A lot of times the best way to hunt was to hold perfectly still and wait for your prey to come in range.

"I'm not living here." Kanvar kept his distance and circled around his father. He could feel Devaj and Denali farther off in the palace.

"Devaj said you have Akshara's memories?" Amar said, voice soft and non-threatening. "Things are very different here than Stonefountain."

"Are they?" Kanvar stopped and glared at his father. "You made the villagers tie me up and leave me on the cliff. Then you came for me, took me prisoner, and brought me here. Locked my mind away, took control of my body. You're no different than Khalid." Khalid had been the Great Gold King a thousand years before at Stonefountain. Amar was his grandson.

Amar's eyes widened in surprise, and his hands twitched. "I never told the villagers to tie you up. They took you to the cliff because you were dying, and the Great Gold dragons are too big to fly down through the canopy. I came to save you, Kanvar. I never hurt you in any way. All I did was numb your mind so you wouldn't hurt while I treated your wounds."

"You tore Dharanidhar's presence from my mind and locked me away from him. Do you think that didn't hurt? It did. I promise you." The memory of losing contact with Dhar's mind made Kanvar shudder.

Parmver coughed. "Well, I'm just going to leave you to work this out." He shuffled past Kanvar and hobbled off across the hall.

Amar swallowed, swayed as if he might step toward Kanvar, but then let out a slow breath and stayed in place. "I did not mean to hurt you. I didn't understand then that you and Dharanidhar were already partially bonded. I knew your minds were linked. That is all. I feared he was hurting you. He's an old and powerful dragon. I wanted to protect you. I'm sorry I blocked you from him. I didn't mean to cause you any pain. Kanvar, please forgive me."

Kanvar wavered. His father sounded so sincere. Devaj had insisted that Amar was a kind and gentle man. "Even if I did forgive you," Kanvar said past a lump in his throat. "How could I ever trust you?"

"You can look into my mind, search it all you want, and see what kind of man I really am. I'll let you do it. No shields, no blocks, nothing hidden. Then if you still don't like me, I'll stay away and leave you alone." Amar held out a single hand in invitation.

Kanvar took a step toward him and stopped. Amar was baiting the trap, luring him in for the kill. *Dhar, what do I do?*

Dhar's mind wrapped around Kanvar's, giving him strength. *I think my mind is as powerful as Amar's. Together we're a match for him and Rajahansa. You don't have to face them alone. We should look. I'd like to know for sure what kind of man he really is. Take his hand and I'll keep you safe.*

Kanvar slid his crossbow into its harness and limped over to his father. A deep memory-fear stirred.

Amar waited perfectly still, hand outstretched, his mind open.

Kanvar bit his lip and hesitated. His gut twisted and his heart beat out of rhythm.

"It's all right," Amar said. "Take my hand and I'll show you everything."

Dhar nudged Kanvar forward. Curiosity ate at him. He wanted to see into Amar's mind and learn the truth about his old enemy.

Kanvar reached his right hand out and pressed it against his father's.

Amar's hand felt warm and comforting. He kept his mind open, but did not wrap it around Kanvar's as he'd done before. It lay in front of Kanvar like an open book on the table, leaving Kanvar to step up to it and turn the pages however he wanted.

Kanvar hesitated.

Dharanidhar snorted, moved forward, and flipped the book open to the very beginning. Kanvar slid into his father's memories like he'd done with Parmver's and Akshara's memories of Stonefountain. Only his father's memories started five hundred years later. He played as a small child in the palace chambers—tag and hide-and-seek and jungle monkey with the young gold dragons.

His parents, both Nagas, were always there for him—his father a king, kind and regal, his mother Parmver's daughter, as beautiful as a jungle flower. They wrapped their love around him and kept him safe until the day they went away to investigate a disturbance on the coast. Some humans had crossed the sea from Varna and were killing the dragons under Father's protection.

Amar was playing in the great hall with Rajahansa when he felt a sudden stab of pain, and his link to his parents was torn away, leaving a gash in his soul. He screamed and screamed until Parmver reached him and soothed the pain. But Amar's parents never returned. The Varnan Naga hunters had killed them.

Parmver raised Amar, trained him to use his powers, helped him to bond with Rajahansa when the dragon sickness took him. Years passed in quiet solitude. Parmver had many other children at the village. Only three of them became Nagas, all boys.

Amar took over his father's duties of guarding and caring for all the Great Dragons in the jungle. Except not the Great Blues. The blues hid in the mountains and tried to kill the golds whenever they could. Parmver told Amar he should leave them alone. The Great Blue dragons did not want Amar to watch over and care for them. They were violent and bloodthirsty, killing even each other as they fought for power among themselves. Amar took Parmver's advice and left them alone.

Parmver spoke to Amar one day while the two of them tended the broken leg of a Great Green dragon. "You should marry," Parmver said as he placed a splint on the leg.

His words startled Amar. "Who?"

"Someone from the village. There are plenty of pretty girls there."

"None of them are Nagas." Amar carefully tied the splint in place.

"Nothing says you have to marry a Naga."

"A human woman would grow old and die, like your wife did." Amar had watched the girls at the village. Many were beautiful and kind, but they worshipped him as their king and did not treat him like the other men of the village.

Parmver patted the green dragon's side. "There you go. You'll need to keep off it for a bit. You're welcome to stay here until it heals."

Thank you, the Great Green dragon rumbled.

Parmver led Amar out of the chamber into the hall. "You are the king. You must have an heir. I am getting old. There are only five of us, Amar. Five Nagas left in the whole world. If you and my sons don't marry and have children, we will die out. The Nagas will be gone forever. Besides, you need human companionship. It's too lonely here. Go to the village and find a wife."

Amar listened to Parmver, and married a village girl. She was beautiful. He loved her. They had six children. None of them Nagas. His wife grew old and died. His children grew old and died. Their deaths left him empty. His grandchildren were not Nagas, and their children were not Nagas.

Parmver urged him to marry again. Again he complied and raised a family. Loved his wife, adored his seven children, did everything for them a gentle father could do. And none were Nagas. All died. Amar swore he would never marry again. His broken heart could not be mended. He stayed away from the village and other humans, spending all his time with the gold dragons, and seeing to his duties as king.

More and more humans were coming across the sea. They set up colonies along the shore, hunted the dragons, chopped down the trees. Amar ordered the Great dragons to withdraw deeper into the jungle. He did not want to fight the humans or hurt anyone.

The Great Blue dragons fought back against the humans. Waging war. Killing and burning. Every time a Great Dragon or human died, Amar felt the pain of their death in his own heart. He tried to convince the Great Blue dragons to stop fighting, but they would not listen to him. The humans had killed Dharanidhar's hatchlings, and Dharanidhar vowed to kill all the humans in revenge.

Amar was horrified by the carnage. He went in disguise to the human colony from Varna, looking for a way to convince the humans to go back to their own lands. From the night shadow of the colony wall, he watched a Varnan boat come to shore. A beautiful young woman sat in the bow of the ship. Her face glowed in the moonlight. The wind ruffled a lily she had tucked behind her ear.

Amar felt something stir inside him, an intense longing like he hadn't felt since he came down with the dragon sickness so many hundred years before. A love so strong he could not breathe as he watched her father step from the boat and give her a hand out. Her father was dressed in armor made from a Great Red dragon hide. The scales glimmered blood red in the moonlight. He carried a sword and a heavy crossbow that looked like it could hold two bolts at once, and shoot with enough force it could take down a Great Blue dragon. Other men jumped out of the boat and secured it to the dock. They called the armored man Raza, Great Dragon Hunter.

Amar withdrew and flew back to the palace. Raza was a hunter like the ones who had killed Amar's parents.

He didn't dare return to the colony. Raza would have a singing stone. If he found out what Amar was, he'd use the stone so Amar couldn't protect himself. He'd kill Amar without a thought.

But the more Amar vowed to stay away, the more intense his longing became for the woman he'd seen on the boat. She haunted his dreams. Her face danced through his mind during the day. He could not focus on his duties. Nothing mattered but her.

Parmver confronted him when Amar put aside his usual robes and donned clothes from the village. "What's wrong with you, Amar?"

Amar's heart beat so loud he thought Parmver would hear it. Amar grinned at the man who had counseled him so often to remarry. "I'm in love."

"With who?" Parmver asked in surprise.

"The Great Dragon Hunter's daughter." Amar got his boots on and stood. "I'm going to see her. Indumauli says they're having a celebration at the colony tonight. There will be music and dancing and . . . Parmver, I have to see her again."

"Are you crazy?" Parmver grabbed his shoulders and shook him. "You can't go to the colony as long as Raza is there. He'll kill you."

Amar pulled away. "I don't care. I'd rather be dead than spend one more moment without her."

"You don't even know her."

"I've seen her. I've felt her presence up close. I can still feel her here with me." Amar rubbed his chest. "I have to go to her, Parmver. I have to."

Ignoring Parmver's continued protests Amar went to Rajahansa and asked his dragon to fly him to the colony. Rajahansa refused. *No good can come of this, Amar.*

"Fine. Don't help me." Amar stormed away and convinced one of the other Great Gold dragons to take him. He snuck into the big house where the colonists were celebrating and found her there. It took him a while to get up the courage, but before the celebration ended he introduced himself to her and learned her name was Mani. They danced. Amar fell more deeply in love than he'd been a few hours before. So in love he allowed Mani to introduce him to her father.

Kumar Raza seemed pleased that his daughter had found a suitor. Amar could not tell if Raza suspected who he was or not. Raza's mind was carefully locked away from him. Most humans had no concept of mind shields or even a glimmer of the idea they should control their thoughts, but Raza did. Amar figured that was because Raza was a Naga hunter, so Amar was very careful not to use any of his powers around Raza, especially not to try to penetrate Raza's shields. That would be a sure giveaway that Amar was a Naga.

Amar stayed at the colony for weeks, spending as much time with Mani as he could. When he was sure that she loved him as much as he did her, Amar asked Kumar Raza for her hand in marriage.

Raza grew quiet and thoughtful. After a heartbeat too long for Amar's liking, he said he would consider the match if Amar proved himself a good enough dragon hunter. Varnan law required that Mani marry within the dragon hunter jati.

Amar recoiled. He couldn't. He'd never killed anything. He was the king, the protector of life in the jungle. He went back to the palace, intending to forget about Mani. But he couldn't force her from his mind. He loved her. But to kill some creature, even a lesser dragon, that would be impossible. Evil.

Amar sickened. He couldn't eat. He couldn't sleep. He wished he were dead himself. Rajahansa came to his chambers and dragged him out to a window overlooking the jungle. *All things die,* Rajahansa said. *Death is part of life. Even we gold dragons need meat to live. To stay alive we kill lesser creatures and eat them. Is that evil? Killing intelligent beings like humans or Great Dragons is wrong. But the jungle is full of hunters. From the swarms of red ants on the ground to the black monkeys in the trees. No one will think poorly of you if you hunt and slay a lesser dragon. You can do this thing.*

"I thought you did not approve of my courting Mani." Amar could not believe his friend and companion was urging him to kill something.

It is dangerous, but I'd rather have you be happy with her than let your loneliness drive you to your death. Kill a lesser green serpent. You know the big one that lives down by the village and has tried time and again to feast on the villagers. It needs to be stopped anyway. Rajahansa held out Amar's golden sword to him.

Amar took it, and its magic wrapped around him. "This sword wasn't meant for killing. It should only be used for the Naga bonding ceremony."

And what good is that if there are no more Nagas left to bond?

"All right." Amar strapped the sword to his waist. "Take me to the village."

Killing the green serpent was all too easy. Amar simply called it out from its lair and struck off its head while it was in thrall to Amar's mind. He took his trophy back to the colony and claimed his bride. He was so much in love he didn't even care that he had to leave behind his palace and all its luxuries and move to Varna. He cherished every moment he spent with Mani, knowing too soon she would grow old and die. But sometimes he had to leave her. The dragon hunter jati council expected him to hunt. He went on many expeditions to Kundiland with Kumar, and found things went far better for the Great dragons while he was there. He could warn the Great ones away from the hunters and call out the lesser dragons. He began to relish his work because it meant he could protect his subjects. He and Kumar became fast friends.

But then . . . then one day Amar went to call on Kumar to wish him a happy birthday. He thrust aside the door hanging and strode inside. "So, Kumar Raza, you've survived another year," he said jovially.

Kumar had his back to Amar. He whirled around. A picture he'd been holding in his hands clattered to the floor. *The Naga,* Kumar thought.

It was the first time Amar had ever seen inside Kumar's mind. In that instant he realized Kumar knew exactly what Amar was. Amar reacted defensively, blasting Kumar's memories away.

Kumar stared at him with blank eyes. Amar's heart somersaulted. He sucked in a sharp breath, shocked at what he'd done. He'd used his power out of control and hurt the mind of his father-in-law, his friend.

"Kumar, I'm sorry," he said. "I'm so sorry." He couldn't leave Kumar like that. The council would notice such blatant Naga handiwork. And he couldn't return his memories to him. There was too much at stake. Amar had a wife and two sons now to think of. The council would condemn them all to death.

Getting control of himself, Amar gently went back into Kumar's mind and gave him a new life and purpose. He would go to the Great North and live among the tribes. He would hunt a Great White dragon. Amar knew the Great Whites were elusive, and Kumar would not find one for many years, if ever. But he set Kumar's mind, so that when he completed his quest his memory of his life in Varna would return. By then Devaj and Kanvar would be grown. By then Amar might have brought himself to tell Mani who he really was. He could take her and the boys to the palace where they'd be safe.

But the day never came when he revealed himself to Mani. Every time he brought up the subject of Nagas, Mani grew vehement and angry, insisting they should all be killed. And then the worst happened. The worst and the best, because Amar had given up any hope of it hundreds of years before. Devaj came down with the dragon sickness while Amar was away hunting, and Mani learned the truth on her own.

Kanvar untangled himself from his father's memories and pulled his hand away. He had no desire to feel the crossbow bolt Mani had shot his father with. He took a sharp breath and wiped tears from his eyes. His father was not the tyrant Dharanidhar thought he was.

"I-I-I'm sorry," Kanvar stuttered.

"I am too." Amar pulled Kanvar into a gentle hug. "I've missed you Kanvar. It hurt so much when I thought you were dead. Thank you for coming back to me. And for bringing Kumar back safely as well. We should go to him. I think he needs us."

"But what will you do if he tries to kill you?" Kanvar started in the direction Parmver had gone.

"I don't know. But I'll be ready for him this time. More careful. More gentle. I may be able to just make him believe that he likes Nagas instead of hating them. Assuming he remembers anything at all. Parmver fears his mind is too damaged to save. His body is alive, but that seems to be all at the moment."

Kanvar's heart sank. It couldn't be that bad. After everything he'd gone through to save Kumar, he couldn't lose his grandfather now.

Chapter Sixteen

As Kanvar neared the chamber where his grandfather had been taken, he heard Parmver and Devaj talking out in the hall.

"Denali's obviously a Naga," Devaj said. "But I don't understand how. He can't be."

"Of course he can." Parmver's raspy voice sounded amused. "Think, Devaj. You know Nagas only breed true if Naga blood flows through both parents. And both you and Kanvar are Nagas. There can be no doubt that Kumar is from Naga lines. His family may have hidden it for generations, but it is there. That's probably why he's such a good dragon hunter. He must have Naga tendencies himself even though he never came down with the dragon sickness."

Kanvar stopped and glanced over at his father. "Grandfather, a Naga?"

Amar shook his head. "He never came down with the sickness, so he couldn't have bonded. He does have an amazing ability to shield his own mind and a knack for sensing where dragons are though."

"Did you know?"

"No, of course not. You saw my memories. It never occurred to me until you came down with the dragon sickness too, and that wasn't so long ago. A more important question is, did Kumar know? I think it's time to find out."

Amar strode over to Parmver and Devaj. "Did you get Eska some cooler clothes?"

"Yes, she's changing." Parmver pointed to a human-sized chamber down the hall.

"Excellent. Come on, Kanvar. Let's see to your grandfather."

Kanvar followed Amar into a chamber that was both vast and cozy. A bed sat on one side along with some comfortable-looking wooden chairs, a table, a desk and other human furniture. An expensive Varnan rug that looked like it had been made by a master of the weaver jati was spread across the floor. Its gold and red threads glimmered in the sunlight, depicting an image of Stonefountain before it fell. There was a stand to hold Kanvar's armor, and hooks on the wall for his weapons.

The larger part of the room was a vast space with room for Dharanidhar to sit, stand, lie, or walk around at will. There was an arched window big enough for Dhar to fly in and out of. Various rocks around the edges gave the space a cave-like appearance. A pond big enough for Kanvar to lounge in rested in a basin between the rocks. And the floor . . . it was the only place in the palace Kanvar had seen that wasn't covered in gold. Instead it was a smooth gray marble.

Kanvar looked in surprise at his father.

Amar shrugged. "Rajahansa and I thought Dharanidhar would like it better that way."

"You made this for him?" Kanvar felt Dharanidhar's surprise mirror his own.

"We wanted you both to feel at home here."

"Kanvar," Denali called from where he stood holding Kumar's hand next to the bed.

Kanvar limped over.

Kumar's eyes were open. Kanvar grabbed his other hand. "Grandfather."

Kumar did not respond. His eyes remained staring into the air. His hand lay unmoving in Kanvar's grip. "Grandfather?" Kanvar set the hand down and reached up to rest his fingers on his grandfather's forehead, trying to sense Kumar's thoughts. He felt nothing. Kumar's mind was blank.

Kanvar pulled his hand back in fright. It was like his grandfather was unconscious even though his eyes were open. His head was wrapped in bandages that covered everything but his face. His seal-skin clothing had been replaced with a white linen robe that left enough bare Kanvar could see the ugly scars on his arms and legs where the snow wolves had savaged them. His broken leg had been re-splinted and wrapped up tight.

Kanvar moved his fingers down to Kumar's throat to feel for a pulse. It was there, strong and steady. Kumar's chest rose and fell with even breathes, but his mind was gone. Kanvar choked and looked over at Denali. "I tried to save him."

Denali lifted Kumar's hand and pressed it against his cheek. "We both did."

Amar came up beside Kanvar and rested his own hand against Kumar's forehead. "He's still alive. That's something. We just have to find a way to reach his mind. I think if we each share our memories with him. That might spark something."

"How?" Denali asked at the exact moment Kanvar was going to say the same thing.

"I can do it," Amar said. "If you'll open your mind to me, I can transfer your memories into his. Kanvar, I know you don't like me in your head, but it might help."

Kanvar shuddered and stepped back. He knew he had to do it to help his grandfather, but the thought of his father's mind crowding into his made him sick.

"I'll go first," Denali said. "I'm not afraid. I want him to remember me."

"What are you doing?" Eska asked as she slipped into the room, wearing a pale gold dress that hung in silky folds from her shoulders to the ground. Her unbraided hair lay smooth on her shoulders and back.

Amar smiled at her. "My dear, you look beautiful. I'm sure Kumar will be delighted to see you in that dress. It was my first wife's wedding dress."

Eska waved her hand in the air. "Just tell me what you are going to do to help him."

"We are all going to share our memories with him. Denali first. Then you, since he knew you most recently. Don't worry. You won't feel a thing. I'll just spill your memories over into his mind. All right?"

"Of course." Eska went over to the bed and put an arm around Denali.

Kanvar inched back another step.

He knew he shouldn't be frightened. He'd seen inside his father's mind and knew he was a good man, but letting his father into his own mind was another matter. Kanvar rubbed his stumpy left arm while Amar placed one hand on Denali's forehead and the other on Kumar's. He stayed that way for a long time.

The room was silent except for a breeze which snuck in through the window and ruffled Eska's dress.

Sweat broke out on Amar's face. His hand trembled as he pulled it away from Denali and moved it to Eska.

Kanvar remembered the headache he'd gotten from just searching for Parmver's mind among those in the palace. Amar had to be using an immense amount of power and concentration to pull a whole lifetime's worth of memories from one mind and implant it in another. Kanvar didn't relish the headache his father would have when he finished.

A good while later, Amar lifted his hand from Eska and motioned to Devaj. Devaj walked over to the bed, but caught Amar's hand before he could lay it on Devaj's forehead. "Take a break. I'll do it myself."

Amar stepped back from Kumar. Took a deep breath and rubbed his head.

Devaj placed his own hand on Kumar's brow and closed his eyes in concentration. Within moments he was sweating and shaking. Amar watched for a bit, then stepped up and placed his hands on Devaj and Kumar to help. They finished the process together, but Devaj looked far too pale.

"Give yourself time," Amar told Devaj. "Soon you'll be as strong as I am. You're still very young. I'll go next."

Kanvar bit his lip while Amar poured his own memories into Kumar's mind. In a moment it would be Kanvar's turn. He steeled himself. He had to do it. Denali punched him lightly on the arm. "Don't worry. It doesn't hurt. I didn't feel anything at all."

"Of course." Kanvar stepped up to Amar and waited. Finally Amar took a deep breath and stepped back.

"Is it working?" Kanvar asked. "Can you contact his mind yet?"

Amar shook his head. "I don't feel anything. But he has a lot of memories now to replace any that were destroyed when his brain was damaged. It may be enough without yours too."

"You know it's not." Kanvar squared his shoulders. "Thanks, but I want you to give him my memories too. He needs them."

"All right." Amar lifted a shaking hand to Kanvar's forehead. "But don't try to fight me. It won't hurt if you just stay calm."

"I'm calm," Kanvar said, but he didn't feel calm.

You'll be all right, Dharanidhar spoke into his mind. *I'm here with you.*

Does that mean he'll get your memories too? Kanvar whispered back.

"No. I won't let that happen," Amar said out loud. With his hand on Kanvar's forehead, he'd heard the conversation between Dhar and Kanvar.

Kanvar winced. Dhar rumbled encouragement.

Amar's mind slipped like oil into Kanvar's. Kanvar tensed, but Dhar reassured him. It didn't hurt, but it felt strange, like someone rummaging through all his personal belongings, pulling out every experience that had been associated with Kumar and taking them away. *Not taking them,* Dhar rumbled. *Just sharing them, like Akshara shared his memories with my father and my father shared them with me.*

Kanvar grew dizzy and disoriented as snatches of his past spiraled through his mind, each feeling for a moment as if they were happening in the present and then fading to be replaced by the next. When Amar pulled his hand away, Kanvar staggered and almost fell.

Devaj caught him. "Easy there, little brother. You're all right. You see, it didn't hurt at all."

"I agree, hurt is not the right word for it." Kanvar rubbed his head. "I think I'm going to be sick."

"You were fighting a bit and far too tense." Amar shook his hands out and rubbed rivulets of sweat from his forehead.

"Did it work?" Kanvar wrapped his fingers around Kumar's hand. "Grandfather?" Kumar did not move. He remained staring at the ceiling even when Kanvar shook him. "Grandfather, wake up. Please."

Kumar remained as if dead.

Devaj pulled Kanvar gently away from the bed. "Easy there, little brother."

Eska sat on the bed next to Kumar, took his hand, and wept. Denali bit his lip and looked away.

"I'm going to see if I can reach him now." Amar placed both of his hands against Kumar's temples and closed his eyes. Denali paced next to the bed.

Kanvar watched his grandfather's face for any sign of life. He remained unmoving. Then his eye twitched. Then nothing.

Amar pulled back. "I can't feel him. Not at all," he said in defeat. "I think he's gone for good."

"No." Kanvar pushed his father aside and pressed his own hand against Kumar's forehead. "He twitched. I saw him. He's still in there somewhere. He's probably just hiding his mind from you like he always has." Kanvar closed his eyes, took a deep breath, and sent his own mind into his grandfather's. Kumar's mind was no longer empty. Memories swirled around Kanvar, his own, his fathers, Devaj's, Denali's and Eska's. They drew him in, and he got lost in them, unable to focus, unsure of who he was.

You are Kanvar. Dhar's mind wrapped around him, reforming and re-enforcing his identity. *You are Kanvar, and you are trying to find Kumar Raza, your grandfather. Move past these memories. We must delve deeper.*

With Dharanidhar's help, Kanvar slipped his mind past the memories on the surface and came up against an empty black wall. *Grandfather.* He pounded on the wall with mental fists. *Grandfather, open up. Let me in. It's Kanvar. Wake up, please.*

An almost imperceptible crack shot across the wall. *Rajan?* Kumar grabbed Kanvar and pulled him down into the darkness.

"Kanvar." Amar's mind wrapped around Kanvar's and pulled him away from Kumar. "You're hurting yourself. Stop."

Kanvar gasped and opened his eyes.

Amar had snatched Kanvar's hand away from his grandfather. A splitting headache stabbed through Kanvar, and his knees buckled. Amar caught him, but Kanvar thrashed his way free.

"He's in there. I felt him. He's alive. You pulled me away too soon." Kanvar steadied himself against the bed and reached for his grandfather.

Amar grabbed his hand again. "Kanvar, we don't want to lose you too."

"Leave me alone." Kanvar fought to free his hand from his father.

"Wait." Denali stopped pacing and rushed over to the bed. He fumbled with the pouch that hung over his shoulder. He got it open and pulled out a Great White dragonstone.

The sunlight reflected through the crystal and threw a rainbow of color on the wall. "I'm just thinking. I noticed the dragonstones seem to be what the dragons use to talk to each other with their minds. Maybe we can use this one to reach my father. He . . . I . . . when I handed it to him after he killed the Great White dragon, that's when he remembered his past life. Of course he forgot who I was, but that's not the point. The point is, maybe this dragonstone will help."

Denali held the stone out to Kanvar.

Kanvar pulled free of Amar and took the stone. It felt frosty-cold and smooth in his hand.

Amar looked over at Parmver. "What do you think?"

"It can't hurt. And Kanvar's right. Kumar is probably not going to come to you after what you did to him. Let the boy try one more time with the stone."

"All right." Amar put a hand on Kanvar's shoulder. "See what you can do, but if I feel like I'm losing you again, I'll pull you back."

"Just give me some time. There's a wall I have to get through." Kanvar lifted the stone to his grandfather's forehead and pressed it in place with his hand. He was shaking and sweating, and his head felt like someone had shot a crossbow bolt through it.

Dhar lent Kanvar some of his own strength. *Concentrate. Just slide straight back to the wall and look for that crack.* Kanvar was glad to have Dhar backing him up. He knew he had felt his grandfather, but for that one terrifying moment it had seemed his grandfather would drag him down into the prison behind that wall. *I won't let you become trapped,* Dhar said. *You go as deep as you need, and I'll hold onto you.*

With Dhar's encouragement, Kanvar went back into his grandfather's mind. The dragonstone focused Kanvar's thoughts and let him slip easily past the swirl of memories that had so confused him the first time. Kanvar reached the black wall, but search as he might, he could not find the crack.

Use the dragonstone, Dhar told him.

Kanvar twisted the long pointed stone so the tip faced the wall, the he stabbed the stone into the blackness. Color exploded around him.

He stood in a chamber on the top floor of a building in the city of Daro, much like the home he'd grown up in. It was a long room, with curtains partitioning off the cooking and eating area from the sleeping areas and a gathering place in the center. A red and brown rug covered the floor. His twin brother, Rajan, stretched out on his side on the rug, his head and shoulders resting on a stack of pillows while they played Dragon Hunter together. The gamebox sat between them. It had adjustable mountains, trees, and water that represented the Kundiland jungle. Both boys had hidden their dragon somewhere on the board while the other wasn't looking. Now they moved their dragon hunter pieces in turns, trying to find and kill each other's dragons.

Rajan made his move and shot his hunter's crossbow straight into the leafy alcove where Kumar had hidden his Great Copper dragon. Kumar eased the foliage aside and saw the dart sticking into his little wooden dragon's heart. He jumped to his feet. "You cheated again, Rajan. You were watching when I hid it."

Rajan laughed. "No I didn't. Quit being such a poor sport."

"Then you must have read my mind."

"Shhh." Rajan pulled Kumar back down and looked around to make sure no one had heard. "Don't talk like that. People don't understand how we can share each other's thoughts and feel each other's pain. It scares them, Kumar. We have to hide it."

"You said you were going to ask father about it."

Rajan's face went red and he dropped his voice even lower. "I tried. He got very angry and hit me. Told me I must never ever speak of it again to anyone."

"But I didn't feel him hit you," Kumar protested, all thoughts of his conquered dragon swept away with worry for his brother.

"I shielded my mind so you wouldn't feel it. I didn't want you hurt." Rajan lifted his shirt to show black and green bruises spread across his chest and down his ribs.

Kumar was horrified. "He didn't, he couldn't, why?"

"I don't know." Rajan smoothed his shirt back into place. "But I do know this. You and I must never let anyone know that our minds are connected. Do you understand me, Kumar?"

Kumar's face burned. He nodded then whispered in his softest voice. "But you have to promise to stop cheating at Dragon Hunter."

Rajan chuckled and tapped his palm against Kumar's forehead. "I don't try to cheat. You just keep shouting your thoughts across the whole room."

"Then teach me to block my mind like you do."

The memory of the Dragon Hunter game spiraled away from Kanvar's mind, replaced by a new memory. Kumar and Rajan were in the courtyard at the dragon hunter jati complex, practicing with their swords. Rajan was far better at the sword than Kumar, though Kumar could outshoot him with a crossbow. But today Rajan was losing. He'd already dropped his sword twice, and had a nice scratch on his left arm from Kumar's blade to show for it.

Kumar made a quick side-thrust, and Rajan failed to block it. Kumar barely pulled back in time to keep from stabbing his brother in the gut. He lowered his sword. "Rajan, what's wrong."

Rajan wiped the sweat from his face and shivered. "I don't know. I can't concentrate. It's so cold today, and I feel like part of me is missing. Like I've suddenly gone all empty inside."

"You can't be empty. I'm here with you." Kumar lowered his mind shields so his brother could feel his presence better. When their minds touched, Kumar felt a jagged crevice in Rajan's heart. "Rajan, what is it?"

"I don't know." Rajan shivered again. "But maybe we should be done practicing for today. Let's go home."

The next morning Rajan couldn't get out of bed. A horrible sin as far as their father was concerned. He said a dragon hunter should always rise early.

"Kumar, Rajan," their father's rough voice called from the center room.

Rajan was shivering and covered with sweat.

"Just a minute," Kumar called.

"Not just a minute." Their father pushed aside the curtain and stormed over to the bed. He took one look at Rajan, and his face turned crimson. "Get up," he shouted. "We're going hunting. There's a boat leaving for Kundiland this morning."

"I thought you said we were too young to go with you on this hunt," Kumar protested. "Besides, I think Rajan is sick. We should call a Unani doctor."

"We most certainly should not. Get up, Rajan." Father jerked Rajan out of bed. "Get dressed and come to the boat." He stormed out and left the building.

Kumar helped Rajan get his armor on and gather his weapons. Neither boy said anything. The fury they'd felt from their father was too terrifying. Rajan grew weaker and weaker during their voyage across the sea, but that did not stop their father from including both boys in the hunt for a Great Green dragon. Their father split them up and sent them in opposite directions to flank the dragon's lair while their father and uncle made a direct approach, hoping to pin the dragon between the four of them.

Kumar eased through the thick jungle growth, crossbow loaded and ready. He was downwind, and there was a good chance the dragon would bolt in his direction if startled. He could feel it stretched out in its lair where it had just eaten a black monkey.

Rajan stalked the dragon from the opposite side.

The crack of a crossbow discharging split the air, and Kumar felt a hot burn between his ribs. He looked down expecting to see a crossbow bolt sticking from his chest. That's what it had felt like, but he was unhurt.

"Rajan!" he shouted.

He sped straight toward his brother, ignoring the Great Green dragon which jumped to its feet as Kumar raced past the mouth of its lair.

Kumar found Rajan slumped at the base of a tree, a crossbow bolt sticking out of his ribs a few inches below his heart.

"No," Kumar swore. He set down his crossbow and pulled out his vial of dragon saliva and his bandages—items every dragon hunter carried with them on a hunt. Too many things could go wrong in the jungle.

"Kumar." Rajan reached a hand out to him. "I don't think you can heal this."

"Of course I can. Lie down." Kumar eased his brother to the ground, jerked the bolt free from his body, and threw it aside. Blood welled up from the wound. He slathered the dragon saliva over it and wrapped it up tight with the bandages. "Stay here. I'm going to get father and tell him there's been an accident."

"No, wait." Rajan said. But Kumar raced away, his heart beating, sweat stinging his eyes. He could feel his father on a little hillock close by but couldn't see him through the trees.

He heard his father and uncle talking ahead.

"Did you do it?" his father asked.

"Yes." His uncle's voice was rough and low. "If he's not dead already, he will be very soon."

"Good. I'll get Kumar and we'll go back to the boat."

Kumar skidded to a stop and flattened himself behind a tree. He couldn't believe what he'd just heard. His uncle had shot his brother on purpose. It wasn't an accident. And his father had agreed to it. Surprise, fear, and anger swept through Kumar. He stood frozen, unable to come to grips with what he'd just seen and heard.

"Kumar," his father called. "Kumar come back. It's too late. The dragon knows we're here now. Let's go."

Kumar didn't answer. He couldn't speak. Couldn't move. Shock and fear consumed him.

"I heard footsteps over there," his uncle said.

Kumar bolted back the way he'd come. He'd left his crossbow next to Rajan. He had to get it. But he was too slow. Just before he reached Rajan, his uncle tackled him and wrestled him to the ground, pinning his arms behind his back.

"Murderer," Kumar shouted. "You shot him. I'm going to tell the council."

"No you won't." His uncle dragged him to his feet and pressed a sword against his throat. "Because if you ever speak a single word of this, I'll slit your throat you little brat. I should do it right now."

Kumar's father stepped out of the trees. "No. You won't kill Kumar. Not unless he gets a fever too."

"But he knows."

"He doesn't know anything." Kumar's father walked over, grabbed Kumar's hair and jerked his head back to look into his face. "Your brother was killed by a Great Green dragon while on a hunt. Do you understand me?"

"No, he wasn't." Kumar said through gritted teeth.

His father struck him across the face. "The dragon killed him, and you will never speak a single word about his fever or anything else, because if you do, the council will kill all of us. The entire family, Kumar. Everyone. Swear by Stonefountain you will keep this secret, or the Great Green dragon will claim two hunters today instead of one."

Kumar shook his head and glanced over to where his brother lay on the ground. Rajan's eyes were closed, but he was still breathing.

His father followed Kumar's gaze and swore. "You missed, Brother. He's still alive."

"It doesn't matter," his uncle said. "If the wound doesn't kill him, the fever will. He'll never wake again."

His father glared at his uncle. "Take Kumar to the boat. Do whatever you must to make sure he promises to keep this secret."

Kumar's uncle started to drag him away.

"No, you can't leave him here to die." Kumar struggled to free himself, but the sword cut into his neck.

"Of course I won't," his father said. "That would be cruel." He lifted his crossbow and aimed it at Rajan.

His uncle dragged Kumar back into the trees where he couldn't see, but he could hear the crack of the crossbow discharging. His father never missed.

Kumar screamed, and Kanvar screamed with him, reliving the memory of his brother's death. It felt like his entire soul ripped away, leaving unfathomable emptiness.

"Kanvar." A strong golden glow wrapped around Kanvar, put his soul back together, and pulled him away from Kumar's mind.

Kanvar opened his eyes and found himself lying on the floor, Amar leaning over him, stroking his forehead. "It's all right, Kanvar. You're going to be fine. Just stay down for a minute." Kanvar was too shocked by what he'd seen to move or protest.

"Rajan!" Kumar's deep voice boomed out across the room. He jerked to a sit and looked around him.

Chapter Seventeen

"Father," Denali shouted with delight and threw himself at his father in a big hug. "Father, you're alive."

Kumar returned the hug and then eased Denali back so he could see his face. He blinked at Denali for a moment as if confused, then a light came into his eyes.

"Denali, what happened to the snow wolves? Where are we?"

Denali puffed out his chest in pride. "Frost and I defeated the snow wolves by ourselves. But then the mountain exploded into a volcano, and Kanvar came and saved us and brought us here to this palace. It's amazing. Huge. All made of gold. And there are dragons everywhere, only they don't want to eat us. And Kanvar's father is a king, can you believe it?" Denali bounced on the bed in excitement. He was so glad to have his father awake and speaking to him.

"Slow down," Kumar said. "I didn't understand half of it."

Eska squeezed his hand, and he looked over at her. "Eska, have you been crying?"

Eska smiled through her tears. "You were hurt. Dying. But Kanvar and the Naga king have brought you back to us."

Kumar followed Eska's glance to the other side of the bed where Amar hovered over Kanvar.

Amar straightened as he and Kumar locked eyes.

"Now, Kumar," Amar said, lifting his hands in a placating gesture. "Don't do anything rash."

Kumar's face went red and he slid to his feet.

"Don't do anything rash?" he shouted. "You slimy, scaly, treacherous, fool of a Naga!" He swung his fist and punched Amar in the face. "Sending me off to the north to hunt a useless Great White dragon. How could you? You ruined everything. If you would have only given me a moment to explain."

Denali's heart froze. He'd been so excited to see his father awake, he'd forgotten Kanvar's warning that Kumar might turn against them the way the Tuniit tribe had.

Kumar's punch sent Amar reeling and split his lip.

Amar steadied himself and pressed a hand against his bleeding lip. "I'm sorry," he said. "I couldn't risk you hurting my sons, and I warn you, if you raise a hand against them now, I'll take control of your mind again. You don't have your singing stone here to stop me."

Devaj helped Kanvar up off the floor, and the two brothers stood together to face the furious Kumar. Denali held his breath.

Kumar lowered his fist and looked the two boys over for a moment, then a smile lit his face. "You've bonded? Both of you? Thank the Fountain." He sank down to sit on the bed, rubbing his broken leg.

Amar cleared his throat. "You're . . . um . . . happy about that?"

Kumar glanced up at Amar and noticed the golden crown across his brow. His smile faded a bit. "So you're a king? I have to admit, I never guessed that part of it."

"King Khalid's grandson." Amar smoothed his robes.

Kumar lowered his head in respect. "I didn't know any of the royal family had survived."

"Bowing is not necessary," Amar said, surprised at the show of respect from Kumar. "But I don't understand. I thought you would try to kill me and the children."

Kumar shook his head and wrapped an arm around Denali's shoulders.

Denali was grateful for the reassurance. He didn't think he could have lived with it if his father had tried to kill him.

"Three Nagas in two generations. Who would have thought?" Kumar said.

"Four, counting Rajan," Kanvar said.

"Who's Rajan?" Denali asked.

Kumar grimaced. "I'll explain if Amar doesn't blast my mind to bits again." He glared at Amar. "I would have told you back then if you had given me the chance."

Amar shrugged. "I'm sorry. It was reflex."

Kumar chuckled. "I'm sure it was. It's a wonder any Nagas have survived at all." Kumar scanned the faces of all the people around him.

Denali was glad to be there with them: his father and mother, the king, Kanvar, Devaj, and Parmver. Kumar seemed pleased as well.

"So are you going to tell us?" Amar asked, folding his arms across his chest.

"Yes, but it's hard. I—" Kumar shuddered.

Kanvar limped forward. "He swore by the Fountain that he'd never speak of it. Of course he had a sword against his throat at the time, so I don't think it could be considered a freely given oath."

"You saw that?" Kumar asked.

Kanvar nodded.

"Will you explain then? I-I don't think I can. It hurt too much." Kumar put his hand to his head, and Eska convinced him to lie back.

Denali listened in horror as Kanvar told them all about Kumar's twin brother and how he died.

Kumar squeezed Denali's hands. "I didn't understand why they killed Rajan until later. After my father died, I was going through his things and I found an ancient journal. I had to break three locks off it just to open the crumbling pages. It was written by a long-ago ancestor. He was the captain of the royal guard when King Khalid ruled at Stonefountain."

"Andonil," Parmver said with delight as if they'd been friends.

"Yes, Andonil," Kumar continued. "The king heard rumors of an uprising in a village on the northern seashore and sent Andonil and his dragon to check on it. But Andonil never made it there. He came down with the coughing sickness and stopped at a small oasis in the desert. He was sick for a long time. When he regained his strength, he went back to Stonefountain and found it overthrown. Shocked, he sent his dragon into hiding, disguised himself as a freed field slave, and searched for any Naga survivors. He found none, and started a new life. Andonil, under his new false name and guise, started the dragon hunter jati. He was sickened by the slaughter of the Nagas and furious at the dragons who had rebelled. He vowed to hunt them all down and kill them."

A faint cry of protest escaped from Kanvar.

Kumar paused and looked up at him in concern.

Amar put a restraining hand on Kanvar's shoulders. "Kanvar is bound to a Great Blue dragon. He's seen what happened at Stonefountain from a different viewpoint."

"I wish someone would tell me what happened," Denali said. "You keep talking about things as if everyone knew." Denali tried not to be irritated. So much had happened long ago that mattered greatly now.

"Don't worry," Parmver said. "I'm going to teach you all about it."

"Kanvar," Kumar said. "Tell your dragon not to eat me. I'm just recounting history the way it was recorded in Andonil's journal. The point is, Andonil was also trying to find any Nagas who survived, and he wanted to help any new ones that might be born. He left an explanation in the journal about the bonding ceremony and how it should be done. After I read the journal, I promised myself I would never kill one of my own children or grandchildren. But I knew they would die a horrible death anyway if I could not find a gold dragon for them to bond with. I hunted for the gold dragons all over the world. When Mani was born, I watched her carefully, fearing she would come down with the fever before I could find the golds. She did not, thank the Fountain.

"Then I heard that a gold dragon had been sighted in Kundiland. I took Mani with me and went, determined to stay until I found what I was looking for. Funny, but it found me, and it was far more than I believed possible." Kumar laughed and looked up at Amar.

"You came walking through my front door all of your own free will. I knew what you were the moment you entered the house. The way you carried yourself. The way you responded to people in conversation a moment too soon, as if you had read their thoughts. And if that hadn't given you away, your smell would have. I recognized it the minute Mani brought you over to me."

"I smell?" Amar said, surprised.

"You smell like molten gold, just like Rajan did when he came down with the fever. I knew what you were, and I also knew that you could not have survived and grown to manhood if you were not very cautious. I didn't want to scare you away, so I shielded my mind from you, never letting you know that I knew you were a Naga. I figured it was enough to have you in the family. If any of my grandchildren or great-grandchildren were

Nagas, you'd be there to help them bond when they came down with the fever. But then you—"

Kumar licked his lips and shuddered. "You came to my house on my birthday. Our birthday, Rajan's and mine. I was thinking of him, and you startled me. My shields were down, and then that was it. My life gone in an instant. You fool. But I forgive you. You have good reflexes. I'm sure that's what has kept you alive."

Amar's brow furrowed. "My parents weren't as cautious, and they died."

A plaintive sob echoed at the back of Denali's mind. He felt Frost curled up on the ice in the ice chamber weeping. Her dead father's dragonstone lay on the bed where Kanvar had dropped it. Denali picked it up. "You're not the only one who has lost your parents. Poor Frost. She can't stay locked up in that room by herself."

"No, of course not," Amar said. "But winter is coming to the mountains soon."

"It can't be," Denali interrupted. "Winter is just ending, we're supposed to have sunlight soon."

"In the north, winter is ending. Down here, the seasons are reversed. When your winter ends, ours begins. Not that it ever gets cold around here. We get a lot of rain though, and up in the tops of the high mountains it does turn to snow. And that is where the Great Blue dragons have made their home. Unless they've moved since I found them. Kanvar?"

"No. The pride is still there. Wary. Guarding constantly against possible attack by your gold dragons, but still there," Kanvar said.

"We have never gone around looking for Great Blue dragons to attack and enslave," Amar said, annoyed.

"I know that now." Kanvar lifted his hand to rub it along his crossbow. "And so does Dharanidhar. Convincing the others won't be easy, but we can try."

"Good." Amar rubbed his hands together. "Then I think Frost should go with you and Dharanidhar up into the mountains."

"I'm going too," Denali said. He didn't want to be separated from Frost.

"No," Parmver objected.

"Yes," Amar said. "For a little while. Just to make sure she's happy. Then Denali and Kanvar can both come back here before the snow falls. They'll spend the rainy season here under your tutelage, Parmver."

Kanvar started to protest, and then stopped. He stood quiet for a moment then nodded. "Dhar thinks that's a good idea. He says his old bones will be much more comfortable here in the winter, and that the pride will raise Frost collectively like they do with all orphans. She won't be alone while Denali and I are away from her. What do you think, Denali?"

Denali grinned. He loved the feel of the hot sunlight on his back and the reassurance that he was surrounded by people who would not turn against him the way the Tuniits had. "I like it here. I want to stay forever where the sun shines."

DRAGONBOUND

Kanvar practiced with his new crossbow while Frost and Denali chased each other around the lake near the cliff where the Great Blue dragons made their home.

"Move your hand up on the stalk a little more." Kumar adjusted Kanvar's grip on the crossbow and nodded for Kanvar to take a shot.

Kanvar pulled the trigger, and the bolt went straight into the center of the target Kumar had fashioned out of Kanvar's old mismatched armor. Kanvar felt comfortable in the new glimmering blue armor he'd made from Dharanidhar's cast-of scales.

"A fine shot," Kumar said.

Kanvar grinned. "Thanks to you." The crossbow his grandfather had made for him was lighter, stronger, and easier to load and fire than his old one had been. Kumar had even carved a Great Blue dragon into the wooden stalk. Kanvar lowered the crossbow and faced Kumar. "I'm glad you're back."

"I'm glad I'm back too. Nothing in the world tastes as bad as seal blubber. Ugh." Kumar made a face, then looked fondly over at Denali and Frost.

"I think they're happy here," Kanvar said.

"Yes, they are." A gentle smile tugged at the corners of Kumar's mouth. "But I, for one, can't wait to get back to the palace. I've had enough cold to last a lifetime. Thank you for finding me and bringing me home."

"You're welcome." Kanvar propped the crossbow against his leg and offered his hand to Kumar.

Kumar took it and then pulled Kanvar into a tight hug. Kanvar hugged him back, feeling perfectly safe and content for the first time since Devaj had come down with the dragon sickness.

Epilogue

Kumar Raza stepped through the doorhanging, leaving behind Daro's dusty streets. He climbed the staircase up to the top floor to the chambers his daughter and Amar had inhabited since they married.

Daro's dry heat was nothing like the humidity of Kundiland or the ice and snow in the freezing north, but Daro had always been home to him before Amar had sent him away. Kumar was glad to feel the sweat running beneath his clothes and smell the sun-baked bricks of the building. He savored the memory of hot bread on his tongue mixed with juicy figs. So much better than raw fish and boiled seal meat. Kumar was glad to be home in

Daro, even for a short time. Denali and Eska waited for him back at the palace, but he couldn't settle there until he fixed things here.

He reached the top floor and hesitated in front of the blue and gold cloth that stretched across the doorway, wondering how Mani would respond to his arrival.

"Who's there?" Mani's voice called from inside. It sounded rough and hoarse, unlike the smooth voice he was used to hearing from his daughter.

Kumar pushed aside the doorhanging and stepped into the main room. Mani was leaning over a large wooden chest beneath the window in the far wall. Kumar recognized the chest as his own, and Mani was tearing at the clasps trying to get it open. She lifted the lid, grabbed Kumar's crossbow, and turned to face him. The look on her face turned from fear to astonishment.

"By the Fountain," Kumar said. "What do you intend to do with that? It's too big for you, and it's not even loaded."

Mani's face went red, and she dropped the crossbow. "Father?" she said as if she couldn't believe he had finally returned after so many years.

Kumar winced as his most prized weapon hit the ground. "We'll I'm not a member of the camel herding jati come to sell you some milk, though you look like you could use some. You're far too thin, Mani." She *was* too thin. Her clothes sagged on her gaunt frame. Her hair hung around her face in stringy snarls. "Have you been skipping meals?"

Mani shuddered. "I can't eat."

"Why not?" Kumar strode across the room, lifted his crossbow from the ground, and returned it to the chest. It appeared all of his valuable possessions had been packed up and moved here. No doubt his own chambers were now inhabited by someone else.

"I just can't. Not anymore. Not since . . ." She slumped into a chair next to the expensive dragonhide-covered table.

"So, you were going to shoot me?"

"No," Mani said in alarm.

"Who then?" Kumar sat in a chair opposite his daughter and took her hand. He could tell the past five years had been very hard on her. At least the jati council hadn't killed her or named her untouchable. She'd kept her standing in the jati, but she didn't look happy about it.

"Him. He keeps sneaking in while I'm gone and re-filling my money chest. I never catch him, but what if someone sees him? They'll come for me for sure."

Kumar had a pretty good guess whom Mani was talking about, but didn't let on just yet. He needed to know Mani's side of the story, to understand what she'd been through and how she felt about Amar now.

"Who keeps giving you money?"

"Amar." Mani's voice cracked.

"And shouldn't he do that? He is your husband."

The last of the color drained from Mani's haggard face. "He's dead. Father, I killed him. I found out he's a Naga, and I shot him with your crossbow. The boys too. I killed them all, loaded their bodies into the cart, took them to the bay and dumped them like every Naga deserves. Death and desecration. Of course the All Council didn't want to believe me, but I showed them the blood. Blood here on the floor where I shot them, blood on the window when the Naga fell. Blood on the street below. And lots of blood in the cart. They had to believe me. I killed them all." She blinked back tears then seemed to realize who she'd been talking to, Kumar Raza, once the head of the dragon hunter jati. She jumped to her feet. "You have to believe me. I killed them. The All Council will tell you."

Kumar kept his grip on Mani's hand, standing with her. He tightened his hold and reached out with his other hand, pushing up the left sleeve of Mani's robe to reveal her upper arm. A three inch scar ran down the inner side. It had been a deep cut, healed over afterward by dragon saliva. "Yes, I'm sure there was lots of blood."

Mani let out a frightened cry, tore away from Kumar, and pulled her sleeve back down. She tried to run, but he grabbed her around the waist and held her until she stopped struggling.

"Mani, my dearest child, be still," he said in a soothing voice, running his fingers through her tangled hair. "I'm not going to hurt you. I know what Amar is. I've always known. Unfortunately, he found out I knew and sent me away, leaving you to deal with this alone. Mani, I'm proud of you." He released her and tipped her chin to look up into his face. "You've done well."

Mani shook her head. "Our family is ruined. You should hear what they say about you, that you are no kind of dragon hunter at all if you can't detect a Naga in your own house."

Kumar chuckled. "I don't suppose you mentioned that they didn't notice Amar was a Naga either, despite all the council meetings he's attended and all the hunts he's been on with members of the jati? No, they never figured it out. But I knew."

"You knew?" Mani's voice cracked. She gripped his arms with shaking hands. "You knew, and you let him take control of me anyway? You let him twist up my mind and my emotions to make me love him?"

Kumar winced inwardly. "I don't think he forced you to love him. I think he loved you with all his heart and courted you like any other man, waiting to see if you would love him as well."

"No." Mani stormed away from Kumar. "It wasn't like that. From the moment I first saw him, the second our hands first touched to dance, he cast an unbreakable spell on me. Even now that he's gone, even after I shot him, I feel it wrapped around my heart. Sleep only brings dreams of him. Food has no flavor. I feel like half of my soul is torn away. That's what he did to me. He made me love him, and I can't undo that."

Mani rubbed the scar hidden under her sleeve. "Even after he flew away, he still controlled me. He made me cut myself and pretend they were all dead. You don't understand how powerful he is."

Kumar rubbed his face. Amar was right, Mani would not come to terms with this easily. "Perhaps you're right." Kumar went to his chest and pulled out the little iron box that housed his singing stone. He did not know why the iron blocked the song, but thankfully it did. Steeling himself, Kumar lifted the lid. A glow sprung to life in the blue crystal, and a faint song stabbed through his brain. He'd asked many of the dragon hunters if they could hear the singing stones' music. All claimed they could not. The stones only sang for the Nagas.

Kumar lifted the stone free of the box and held it out to Mani. "The singing stones can break any compulsion put on a person by a Naga. Any spell. Any control of your mind. If that weren't the case, the slaves would not have been able to rebel at Stonefountain. Their minds were enthralled to the Nagas, the way you say yours is to Amar. Here. Take the stone. Break his hold on you."

"Are you sure?" Mani reached for the stone with a shaking hand.

"You know it's true. You've been taught that since you were a child. The dragon hunters carry the singing stones so they will always be safe if they confront a Naga." Kumar pressed the stone into Mani's hand.

Mani winced.

"Do you hear the song?" Kumar said, concerned. He hadn't meant to hurt her with it. She still did not know that she had Naga blood.

"No. Of course I didn't. What are you saying? I am no Naga."

"Of course you aren't." Kumar left the stone in Mani's hand and went back to the chest. He found what he was looking for at the bottom, buried under his armor and other possessions. It was a small wooden box, bound with heavy chains and locked with a combination lock only Kumar knew how to open.

"You have the stone," he said to Mani as he worked the intricate lock. "Now tell me, how do you feel about Amar? Do you hate him the way you should?"

Mani didn't answer.

Kumar glanced up from the lock to see her face. Tears streamed down her cheeks. She mouthed Amar's name, but no sound came out. Kumar turned his attention back to the lock and let his daughter work through her emotions. At least while she was holding the stone, she could be sure the feelings were her own.

Finally Kumar got the lock open, removed the chains, and opened the box. Andonil's tattered journal lay inside, the pages yellowed and crumbling along the edges. "You know our ancestral line," Kumar said. "You have it memorized all the way back to Stonefountain. Our first ancestor is?"

"Dhawal." Mani refused to look Kumar in the face. She stared at the stone in her hand as if it were broken.

"Correct," Kumar said. "Dhawal. That is the name he gave himself after Stonefountain fell, and this is his journal." Kumar crossed the room and held the book up in front of Mani's face. "I want you to read it."

Mani blinked the tears out of her eyes so she could see the journal. "Now?"

"Yes, right now."

"But the stone isn't working." Mani rubbed the singing stone and held it up to the bright morning sunlight that blazed through the open window. The air rippled with movement outside, but she didn't notice it. "I don't feel any different. Surely the stone should have broken his hold on my heart."

Kumar cleared his throat and put an arm around Mani's shoulders. "Amar never used his powers on you. I would have known it if he had."

"How could you?"

Kumar took the singing stone and returned it to its iron prison. He eased the journal into Mani's hands in place of the stone. "Read this. The language has changed some since it was written, but that's why I made you study the ancient language when you were young. Remember how you yelled at me and threw your study book on the ground when you first started?" Kumar laughed. "You were such a fiery little girl." He hoped to see some of that fire come back into her eyes. It hurt him too much to see her defeated like this.

Mani slid into a chair and opened the journal. It wouldn't take her long to read through it. Andonil had not been a wordy man. While she read in silence, Kumar retrieved Mani's travel trunk from the sleeping area and started loading it with the possessions she cared about most. Her favorite clothes and books. He knew her well; she had been his only child. The paintings she loved, the china dishes she treasured, and the bedspread her mother had made for her before passing from life.

"What are these names?" Mani's voice startled him. He closed the trunk, locked it, and pushed it up against the windowsill along with his own trunk. She'd reached the end of the book and found the nine names written in the back. Rajan was the last on the list.

"Rajan was my twin brother," Kumar forced himself to say. The jagged hole in his soul where his brother had been ripped away had never fully healed. "He was a

Naga, and my father killed him. The others were Nagas as well. One almost every-other generation. All murdered to keep the family secret. Killed so that the rest of us could live. But I swore I would not do that to any of my descendants. Rajan will be the last to die at the hands of his own parents.

"I looked long and hard to find the Great Gold dragons, Mani. I never would have gotten captured by a Great Red dragon or battled a Great Silver serpent or had any other of the adventures that made me famous if I had not been in pursuit of the gold dragons. I had to find them before another Naga was born into this family. And I did find them . . . all right, Amar and his Great Gold dragon found us, but the outcome is the same. Your sons are not dead. Both have grown to manhood because Amar was around to keep them alive. In fact, it was Kanvar who saved my life just recently and brought me back from the Great North."

Mani closed the book and handed it back to Kumar. "I have Naga blood in me?"

"Yes." He hoped she would understand. By Stone-fountain, he needed her to be able to accept this truth. He didn't want to lose her.

Mani slipped over to Kumar's chest and pulled out his jungle knife. The steel glinted in the sunlight as she lifted it to her throat. "I'm sorry, Father. Our laws are clear. All Nagas must die. They can't be allowed to return and enslave the world." She moved her hand, intent on slicing the blade across her throat, but Amar catapulted in through the window, grabbed her, and squeezed her hand so she dropped the jungle knife.

"Mani, No," Amar said, holding her tight against his chest.

"But I can't stay here?" she cried. "I can't live with this. The All Council will find out. They'll come for me and burn me, and I don't want to die like that."

"You don't have to die, Mani." Amar leaned down and kissed her on the forehead. "And you don't have to stay here. We spent a long time living together in Daro, because it is your home, but I'd like to take you back to my home now. Somewhere you will be safe, and we can be a family again. I love you, Mani. Will you please come to Kundiland with me?"

Kumar held his breath. He could fight all kinds of battles, but not this one. The outcome would be determined by his daughter.

"But you are a Naga," Mani said.

"I'm sorry I didn't tell you," Amar whispered and stroked her cheek. "I wanted to. Every single day. But I was too frightened of losing you. Will you forgive me? Can you love me anyway?"

In answer, Mani reached up and pulled his head down so she could kiss him.

"Hey." Devaj appeared on the windowsill. "There's a line of clouds blowing in. If we don't leave now, the dragons are going to be visible. Not a good thing this close to the dragon hunter jati complex, don't you think?"

Kumar grimaced and wondered how many dragon hunters the golds could hit with their joy breath at once.

Mani pulled away from Kumar and grabbed Devaj in a hug. "You're alive. Thank the Fountain, you're alive."

"Of course I'm alive. Can we go now?"

"Yes," Mani said. "I think we'd better."

Devaj's dragon reached in through the window and snatched up the two chests. A little more gently, Rajahansa lifted Amar and Mani up onto his neck. Kumar joined Devaj on his dragon. The four humans and two dragons flew westward away from Daro and came safely at sunset to Kundiland and the golden palace.

REBECCA SHELLEY

About The Author

Rebecca Shelley loves adventuring and spent a lot of time in her youth doing things like dog sledding, hiking, camping, and horseback riding. She has a special fondness for dragons and fairies and wrote her first book in Elementary School. To learn more, visit her website at http://www.rebeccashelley.com.

ΔRAGONBOUND

Coming Soon:

Dragonbound: Copper Dragon

Raahi sees a vision of his homeland's most sacred burial grounds desecrated by the conquering Maranies. He and Kanvar head to Darvat to stop the destruction, but come up against a powerful mining corporation, General Samdrasen, and the entire Maran army. They'll need the help of a Great Copper dragon to succeed.

Now Available:

Firebird

Young Aedus of the Nanuk Clan knows nothing of the war between the spirits or the Firebird. Aedus wants only to prove himself a man in the Great Hunt. But when the battling spirits threaten to destroy his clan, he risks everything—not just his life, but his very humanity—to save his people.

REBECCA SHELLEY

Tablet of Destinies

When Tiamat steals the Tablet of Destinies from Anu, the sky god, Gidd, Anu's youngest servant is sent in human form to infiltrate Tiamat's realm and retrieve the Tablet. Gidd's rash actions embroil the young priest, Ber-chan, in the quest with him. Captured and sold as slaves, Gidd and Ber-chan go on a harrowing journey, face terrifying monsters, and confront Tiamat herself in the depths of the sea. Like in the great epic of Gilgamesh, only one of them will return alive, but the destinies of all men and gods depend on their success.

Black Dragon
Twelve-year-old Weldon is a gifted artist, but when his drawings of fairies and dragons come to life, he finds himself caught between some deadly criminals and the jewels they want. Only his dedication and imagination can save him and his friends.

Mist Warriors
The mist on Lake Tahoe holds powerful and dangerous secrets. When Robby's sister vanishes into the mist, Robby follows and finds himself entangled in an ancient struggle between magical foes. Only courage and loyalty can bring him and his sister out alive.

Preview

Mist Warriors

Chapter One

Robby's rollerblades clicked against the cracks in the damp sidewalk as he raced along the dark street far behind his older sister, Ellen. Mist swirled around him, chilling his skin and carrying the scent of the wet pine trees that lined the road. Ellen flitted ghost-like in and out of the swirling patches of mist illuminated by the streetlights.

Robby tried to keep his skates quiet, so Ellen would not notice her younger brother behind her.

Spying.

For the third morning in a row Ellen had gotten up before sunrise, strapped on her purple rollerblades and skated off into the mist without telling anyone. Robby and Ellen usually skated together since they'd moved from Los Angeles to Lake Tahoe and left all their friends behind.

Frowning, Robby followed Ellen as she sped down the steep hill toward the waterfront. She had skated off without him, and he wanted to know why. A pale glow from the streetlight glimmered off a white bandage on her hand and the smooth face of the cell phone clipped to her belt.

Robby pushed himself to keep her in sight.

The sidewalk flashed past beneath his speeding feet. He shivered, and his heart beat hard in his chest. The dark mists made him nervous, not to mention his sister's odd behavior. He swallowed a lump in his throat. Everything felt wrong this morning like a spinning top, tilting to one side before the final crash.

Ellen skated down Village Boulevard to the beach where Lake Tahoe lapped against the wooden pier that stretched out into the dark water.

Robby stopped at the playground and ducked behind the slide, panting to catch his breath.

Ellen took off her skates, walked across the playground sand, and onto the pier. Thick mist swirled around her, coming off the lake. She stood silent and alone, staring across the water.

Minutes ticked by.

Robby wondered what she was doing. Usually when he came down to the lake, he brought his fishing pole. But Ellen hated fishing. She thought it was cruel to the fish. Not Robby. His hands twitched for his pole, but he'd left it home, and for some reason even the thought of fishing in the mist filled him with dread.

Ellen just stood there waiting as fingers of clouds wrapped around her while the first faint glow of sunlight turned the mist ghostly white.

She stood silent and alone for so long that Robby's feet fell asleep and started to prickle. He leaned down to take off his skates, wiggled his toes around so blood would get to them, then put the skates back on.

"What are you doing here?" Ellen's voice made him jump.

Robby looked up in shock. Ellen had come back from the pier and stood a few feet away, glaring at him through the dim half-dawn light. Robby got a hold of himself and glared back. Ellen was seventeen and he only fifteen, but what he lacked in age he made up for in size. Last time they'd measured against each other, he was three inches taller.

Not wanting to admit he'd been spying, Robby pushed back from the slide and sped away. "Race you home," he cried.

Ellen came after him.

Skating down the slope to the beach had been easy. Going uphill was a different matter. Fire burned in Robby's legs as he pumped faster and faster. He gasped for breath, hearing her close behind him.

"Robby, you brat," Ellen said. Her fingers swiped the back of his shirt.

Robby put on a burst of speed, zipped onto Lakeside Boulevard, and up to their home behind a rustic old church.

Ellen came up beside him breathless. "You followed me."

"Sure." Robby leaned over, waiting for his muscles to stop burning and trying to catch his breath. "What were you doing on the pier at this time of morning? It's creepy out there."

Ellen cleared her throat and pursed her lips. For a second he thought she might tell him, but then she pushed off on her skates.

"Race you around the church," she called.

She vanished into the mist.

"Cheater!" he yelled. "You better say what you were doing at the lake, or I'll tell mom and dad you snuck out." Robby sped after her, taking the shorter route around the other side of the church.

He wove past the pine trees, slapped the wooden corner of the church as he went around it, and skated into the parking lot, expecting Ellen to get there at the same moment.

She never arrived.

Robby ground his teeth. The mist had grown so thick it hid the walls of the church behind him.

"Ellen?" he called.

Only the dull throb of a car engine, motoring along Lakeside Boulevard, answered him.

"Ellen?" Robby skated closer to the church to see if she was hiding against one of the walls. A low wind moaned through the pine trees. Robby shivered.

The church walls stood empty.

"Ellen," Robby called. "Ellen."

Silence.

Chapter Two

Six weeks later Robby crept out into the morning mist, and a shiver ran down his spine. Not wanting to wake his parents, he eased the front door closed behind him.

They'd forbidden him to go out alone since Ellen's disappearance. When she'd first vanished, he'd thought she had just ditched him. He had been hurt and angry, but hadn't ratted on her to his parents. He regretted that.

Ellen had never returned.

Robby mounted his bike and retraced his path around the church like he had every morning since he lost her. Silence closed in on him. The damp air stifled his shallow breaths. Fear pulsed through him as the fingers of mist wrapped around his bare neck and brushed his face.

On the far side of the church, he found the parking lot empty. Again.

No Ellen.

Hating himself, he left the church and rode down the slope toward Lake Tahoe. He couldn't get Ellen's last morning out of his mind. She'd gone to the beach, walked onto the pier and stood there waiting.

For what? He didn't know.

He should have told his parents the moment she'd disappeared. They could have called the police. Maybe they would have found her if Robby had told them sooner that she'd gone.

Robby skidded to a stop in the sand and glared at the mist-shrouded water. He shouldn't be out here. He knew that. His fear of the swirling clouds that had claimed his sister made his gut ache. But he'd let her go into that mist; he had to find her. Guilt filled his mouth with a sour taste.

He picked up a rock and hurled it out over the water. It vanished into the mist. A dull splash wafted back to him.

Something in Robby's gut told him whatever she'd been waiting for was connected somehow to her disappearance. Fear of what horrible things might have happened to her clawed his mind.

The police, family, friends and neighbors had scoured Lakeside Village for weeks, looking for Ellen and not found her.

Robby pulled a wrinkled paper from his pocket. The police had given out hundreds of them in the search for Ellen. It showed her with her arms wrapped around a man in his early twenties. Robby's mother had found the picture in Ellen's room. Robby's skin crawled. He and

Ellen were close, but she'd never mentioned the man, and Robby had never seen him before.

The police found and arrested the guy. His name was Warren Gray. He claimed to be Ellen's fiancé and insisted he didn't know what happened to her.

Robby gritted his teeth and glared at the paper. Warren didn't seem like Ellen's type. Dressed in black leather, with his hair long and braided, he looked like some gang member. Robby had always teased Ellen that she was such a prissy princess, if she ever married it would be to some kind of handsome prince.

Ellen had always smiled when he said that.

Now Ellen had vanished, and the police thought this man had killed her. Robby shuddered. Heavy pine scent mixed with the smell of the cold mist. Water lapped at the shore. He refused to believe it. He told himself if he just kept looking, someday he'd find her safe and sound.

Besides, if Warren were responsible, how come three others had disappeared since his arrest?

Mr. Rope who owned the rowboat rental at the dock had left his wife one morning to go to the lake and had never come back.

Brian, a three-year-old who lived up on Crest Lane, had followed his father out into the mist-filled yard. His mother had run right out to grab him only seconds later, but couldn't find him.

Mrs. Candle, the ancient librarian who had glared at Robby every time he entered the library, had set out to get an espresso to start her day and had never been seen again.

The police were baffled. They claimed the disappearances were not related. Robby knew one thing for sure. All of the missing people had gone out into the morning mist and vanished.

Frowning, Robby wiped his hands on his jeans. He'd looked everywhere for Ellen. Each time his search brought him back here to the lake. But the pier sat empty. Mist hung over the deserted beach. No sign of Ellen. Time to go home before his mother woke and found Robby gone too.

He lifted his bike from the sand and brushed the seat off. A movement out of the corner of his eye stopped him from mounting and riding away. The mist over the narrow wooden pier grew darker and denser.

Robby blinked. A kid stood there.

To get to the pier, he would have had to walk right past Robby, yet Robby had not seen him before.

In the thick fog, the kid seemed to be wearing tan leather armor with green swirls on it and a sword hanging at his side. His long blond hair hung to his shoulders. He looked for all the world like a fantasy warrior from one of the computer games Robby's father had created.

Robby rubbed his eyes and squinted through the mist to get a better look.

The kid walked along the pier to the beach. The thick mist followed him. He stepped onto the sand and almost collided with Robby who stood frozen, clutching his bike.

"Hey, watch where you're going," Robby said.

Up close Robby saw that what he'd taken for leather armor was no more than a black leather jacket with silver studs. Despite the kid's long hair, he didn't look any older than Robby.

The black-leather kid dropped into a fighting stance and pulled a fishing knife from his belt.

Robby tensed as the mist licked the wicked blade. He'd used a knife like that often enough to gut fish, but in this boys hands it seemed a lot more menacing. Robby might have expected to get mugged back on the streets of L.A.—before his father made his first million writing that computer game program—not at a resort village in Tahoe.

But people had disappeared, and Robby had felt the evil lurking in the mist. Now he'd come face to face with it. Robby glared at the kid and held his ground. "You going to stab me with that?" If this kid had hurt Ellen, Robby would make him very sorry.

"Who are you?" The kid tried to make his voice sound low and menacing, but it cracked on the last question.

"My name is Robby Chylde. Who are you?" Robby swept the ground with his fingers, grabbing a handful of sand to throw in the kid's eyes if he attacked.

"Greenleaf," the kid snapped. "What are you doing here? What did you see?"

Keeping his eye on the knife, Robby answered. "I'm looking for my sister, and the only thing I've seen today is you. You wouldn't know anything about anyone disappearing, would you?"

Greenleaf took a step back, a look of confusion on his face. "I . . . my brother is gone. Vanished. I came here to look for him."

Robby choked. Not another person lost to the mist.

Greenleaf pointed the knife at Robby. "What have you done with him?"

Chapter Three

"**W**hat have *I* done?" Robby said, edging away from the sharp blade. "I don't even know your brother."

Greenleaf's face flushed. "You. Your people. I know he was mixed up with you."

Robby's heart beat hard, but he knew he couldn't let Greenleaf see fear in his eyes. "I'm not a part of no gang." *Any gang, Robby darling*, his mother's voice echoed in his mind. He shoved it aside, needing to sound tough.

"Gang?" Greenleaf rolled the word on his tongue like he'd never heard it before. He had a strange accent that Robby couldn't place.

Robby narrowed his eyes and said, "You're nuts." Keeping his face toward the knife-wielding boy, he wheeled his bike back toward the picnic tables and playground.

Greenleaf leaped around Robby in a fluid motion, blocking Robby's way. "Where is he?" he said, waving the knife in Robby's face more desperate than menacing.

"I don't know what happened to your brother," Robby said. "My sister's missing too. I told you that. If I knew who took her, do you think I'd be hanging around this beach? No way. I'd do whatever it took to get her back."

Greenleaf's face pinched with fear. "No, he has to be here. My brother said he was going into the human world and not to follow him. But he never came back. If humans are vanishing too then . . . " Greenleaf glanced toward the pier where the morning mist started to thin.

He ran back the way he'd come.

Human world? Robby puzzled over that for a split second then bolted after the crazy kid. The sand gave way beneath his feet, slowing him.

Greenleaf reached the pier, and his feet thumped across the wood. The mist along the beach came to swirl and condense around him.

Robby thundered onto the wooden planks after him. The mist grew thick and cold. Greenleaf was almost to the edge. Robby could barely make him out in the thickening mist.

"Wait," Robby called.

Greenleaf muttered something and kept running toward the water as if he planned to run right off the edge of the pier.

Robby dived for him and caught hold of the back of his jacket just as he stepped off the pier.

Greenleaf's momentum dragged both of them over the edge toward the water below. Robby gritted his teeth against the pending impact, but the fall lasted longer than he expected. Down and down he went, with thick gray mist all around him. Greenleaf's jacket turned from black to tan under his hands.

They splashed into a soggy swamp with long brown grasses shrouded in the dark mist.

Greenleaf screamed in rage, rolled out of Robby's grasp and jumped to his feet. In his hand where the knife had been, he held a sharp sword. The studded black leather was gone, replaced by the fancy armor Greenleaf had been wearing when he first appeared in the mist.

Greenleaf glanced around them in a state of utter panic. "You fool," he screamed at Robby. "Look what you've done." He took a step in the direction that should have been toward shore.

The mist thinned, though the air still hung in a strange half-light. Above him, all Robby could see was gray haze. A swamp spread around him with twisted brown trees. Eerie, glowing moss hung from their branches.

Greenleaf lifted his feet, and the swamp ooze sucked and smacked with each step. After several steps, he whirled and struggled back the way he'd been running when Robby tackled him.

Robby followed, his heart sinking. The end of the pier should have dropped them into Lake Tahoe's cold, clear waters. It was an easy swim from there to shore. But this swamp couldn't be the lake. They'd gone somewhere else, somehow. Robby's mind screamed that it couldn't be true. This had to be a dream.

His senses disagreed. The decaying smell of the swamp and the feel of the cold air against Robby's face made it all too real. He had fallen into a different world.

Greenleaf was trying to get back, but failing. The farther they went, the deeper the swamp became.

When the muck reached their knees, Greenleaf stopped and filled the air with a ragged cry of despair. His despair turned to anger, and he rounded on Robby.

"You idiot," he cried. "I should kill you. Because of you, we're stuck here." He raised his sword.

Robby's muscles tensed, ready to dodge the blow. Then he noticed Greenleaf's hand shook so much he almost dropped the sword. Robby reached up and lifted it from Greenleaf's cold fingers. "I think it would help if you told me where we are," Robby said, "and what you are, if not human."

Made in the USA
Lexington, KY
08 March 2013